MW01132884

To
Jim Robenson &
Family

God bless,

Katie D. Watson

Peter Falls for Nessie

By

Katie S. Watson

authorHOUSE™

1663 LIBERTY DRIVE, SUITE 200
BLOOMINGTON, INDIANA 47403
(800) 839-8640
WWW.AUTHORHOUSE.COM

This book is a work of fiction. People, places, events, and situations are the product of the author's imagination. Any resemblence to actual persons, living or dead, or historical events, is purely coincidental.

© 2005 Katie S. Watson. All Rights Reserved.

No part of this book may be reproduced, stored in a retrieval system, or transmitted by any means without the written permission of the author.

First published by AuthorHouse 09/07/05

ISBN: 1-4208-2534-8 (sc)

Printed in the United States of America
Bloomington, Indiana

This book is printed on acid-free paper.

Dedication

Dedicated with love to the memory of Rev. Gilbert H. Watson; beloved husband, father, grandfather and great grandfather.

'…….God testifying of his gifts: and by it he being dead yet speaketh..' Hebrews ll:4

****

Special thanks to my very good friend Cris Batson, without whose help my manuscript would still be in the computer and not on a disk. Thanks also to Tammy Day who took time to edit my embryonic work Thanks to my son Thomas for the drawings that gave enlightenment to the chapters. Many thanks to Mary and Becky my daughters for their encouragement and help. Thanks to Nick and Beverly Nicholson for the 'Video Eye' that enabled me to see to write my manuscript. Endless thanks to those who will read and hopefully enjoy Peter's experience.

Katie

'Oh, that's the best explanation
you can give, is it?'
'Well, sir, what is yours?'
'The obvious one, that the
    creatue exists.'

Arthur Conan Doyle; The Lost World

'Nessie Watchers
(Loch Ness)

'They sought it with thimbles
They sought it with care;
They pursued it with forks and hope.
They threatened its life with railway shares
They charmed it with smiles and soap.
Lewis Carroll; The Hunting of the Snark

WRITTEN WITH THE FOLLOWING IN MIND

Grandchildren   Great-grandchildren

Faith.................. Timothy C.; Trevor

Timothy...............Brittany; Trey; Katlyn; Cara

Danny......................... William; Maggie; Molly

Jeannie................ Alex; Andrew; Aiden

Phillip, II.............. Greyson

Alex

Scott

Neil

Stephanie .... Dacia; Heylee

Grayson

Hamilton

Cameron

April

Ashley

J. Phillip

Valerie..................Ocean

Mark, II

Cathy……………….. Sarah; Jennifer

Stephen………………Hannah Grace

Timothy A.

Great Grandchildren

Timothy C.; Katelyn; Brittany; Trevor; Trey

Alex, Aiden, Andrew

Dacia   Heylee

Sarah   Jennifer

Author; Ocean; Valerie

Greyson

William, Molly, Maggie

GLOSSARY

Ain	own
Agin	again
AWA	away
Auld	old
Aye	yes
Anither	another
Aroon	around
Aft	after
Aye	yes, o.k.
Aff	off
Aboot	about
Aboon	above
Bairn	child
Blether	talking nonsense
Brither	brother
Bum	buttocks
BRAW	pretty; grand
Ca'd	called
Canna	can't
cannie	cautious
cauld	cold

xi

claise	clothes
clath	cloth
claw	scratch
clootie	(deil) the devil
couldny	couldn't
daft	crazy
dinnie	dinnie, dinna don't
drap	drop
doon	down
faither	father
fleabox	bed
gie	give
goin	going
greetin	crying
hame	home
hoose	house
hen	dearest
isny	isn't
ither	other
ken	know
laddie	small boy
lassie	girl
mither	mother
naw	no
noo	now
och	exclamation
oor	our
pay	salary
scunner	disgusting person
telly	television
tis	it is
telt	tell; told

whisht	quiet
wi	with
wid	would
widny	wouldn't
yer	your
yersel	yourself

Chapter 1

"Peter, when you've finished packing bring your suitcase down the stairs and put it with Alison's and Jamie's. Dad's gone to fill the car with petrol and wants us to be ready to go as soon as he gets back. He hates fighting morning traffic, so be a good lad and get yourself down here in a hurry

"Peter, did you hear what I just said?"

Peter Ellison Maitland at that moment was stretched across his single iron bed, sobbing into a pile of underclothes, socks and shirts his mum had laid out for him to pack. "I don't want to go, and they can't make me," he sobbed to the unpacked mound.

"Peter, did you hear Mum?" The voice and figure of his twelve year old sister Alison entered his room. "Whatever's the matter? Why are you lying on top of your pressed clothes? Why aren't you packing?" she demanded.

1

"Nothin's the matter; just leave me alone. And for your information, I'm not going and they can't make me."

"Oh so you're not going, glared an angry Alison down at her red-faced brother. Hands on skinny hips, she spat out her words in staccato-like formation. "You're daft, you know that? Where do you get off saying you're not going? What do you think Dad'll say when you hand him that bit of defiance? How far do you think it'll get you?"

"I don't care," snapped Peter but with less rancor. The thought of dispensing his decision to his father brought him no great comfort. "I'm just not keen on spending a week with an old aunt and uncle in the wilderness with nothing to do," he whined.

"Pe-e-ter, you should be ashamed. Auntie Mary and Uncle Sam are our dearest kinfolk and you know it. Look at all the birthday and Christmas presents they send us every year. They'll see that we have a good time. There'll be lots to do; explore the Highlands, watch for deer, go fishing, and even...(here her eyes grew big with anticipation), watch for the monster in the loch."

"You and your monster," Peter spat out disgustedly at his sister, but before he could continue the sound of ascending feet galvanized both brother and sister to action. When Mrs. Maitland entered the room, Alison was in process of closing Peter's brown canvas suitcase and Peter was looking under his bed presumably in search of some missed or needed item.

"Did he pack his sponge bag, Alison."

"I didn't notice, Mum."

"Peter?"

"No, I forgot. It's in the loo cupboard. I'll fetch it."

"No, Alison will."

Alone with her son , Agnes sensed a problem. "What's the matter luv?"

"I dinna want to go to Inverness, Mum. I'd rather stay with you and Dad and let Jamie and Alison go by themselves. Summer vacation's almost over and I'd rather spend the rest of the time here in Glasgow with my friends. Please, Mum, please don't make me go."

Agnes heard his words, divined his true feelings and was upset. Peter didn't want to leave the sheltered security of his home. This would be his first time away from her. Uncertainty was gripping him like a vice, and he was reaching out to her as his last hope of deliverance

Alison returned with the sponge bag. Mrs. Maitland inspected its contents: brush, comb, toothbrush and paste, soap and washcloth. Satisfied, she drew the strings closing the bag and handed it to Alison murmuring. "Put it in Peter's case and take it down the stairs like a good lamb."

Alison opened the case wide enough to slide in the sponge bag but not wide enough for her mum to see the jumbled mess of clothes; the result of hurried packing. Closing the case, she went downstairs leaving Peter and his mother alone.

Agnes gathered her small, flushed son to her bosom; stroking his tousled hair she murmured. "It's only for a week luv. A week's not so long. You can phone us a couple of times at evening rates during the week. You'll have the time of your life, you'll see. Before you know it, you'll be home telling us what a grand holiday you had."

Agnes Maitland had anticipated Peter's reluctance to leave her when her husband's brother and sister-in-law had written asking that the children spend a week with them in July before school took up. "He's too wee to go, Alan" she'd argued with her husband. However, when Sam and Mary sent money for the train fares, Alan was adamant about the children honoring the invitation.

"Sam's my only brither. He and Mary are anxious to give the bairns a good time. They've doted on them since they were born. I'll not disappoint them nor insult their generosity because of Peter's infantile hang-up over leavin' his mither."

When Alan used Scottish vernacular for argument's sake, his wife knew it was foolhardy to get him to change his mind.

Agnes listened impatiently as the well-worn dialogue poured out of Alan's mouth. "Peter's nine going on ten. When I was his age I was hustling papers and helping my dad in the garage and garden. He's not anxious to do anything on his own. He clings to you like a leech. Decisions he should be making in school he leaves up to you to make for him. It's time you loosened your apron, took it off, and let him fend a little on his own."

Agnes flushed at her husband's assessment of the troublesome situation. She knew that to some extent he was right. She'd have to give him that.

The horn blew announcing the return of Alan Maitland. Giving her son a firm hug, she turned him around, marched him toward the stairs and stated. "There's Dad, now on you go."

The front door burst open as Agnes and Peter descended the stairs. Peter refused to glance up but kept his eyes riveted on the green carpeted stairs. He examined every worn place lovingly as if this would be the last time he'd ever tread them again. His head bowed to his chin, Peter was the personification of abject misery.

The six foot ex-rugby player that was the father, filled the small hallway. Upon entering, he demanded..."We're all ready, eh. Well, let's be off. Jamie lad, take those cases and follow me to the car; the boot's open." The father's demands left no room for questions they were not in the form of inquiry, but rather in declarative action.

Jamie followed his father, carrying two of the cases. His was an excited exit. He was looking forward to the train trip to Inverness.

Returning from the car, Alan hurried his family out of their small brick bungalow. "Come on, come on, let's be off," he urged. "And for goodness sake Peter, wipe that glum off your face. You'd think you were on your way to the dentist's instead of a train trip to visit your aunt and uncle."

The boot of the 1980 maroon Rover was standing open. Alan inspected Jamie's luggage arrangement, was satisfied and closed the boot with a loud bang. "All in," he ordered.

The three children quickly settled themselves in the backseat with Peter in the middle; for once not complaining about not sitting near a window. With his wife in the passenger's seat, Alan put the key in the ignition, the gears in neutral and turned around to face his children. "Lock your doors; fasten your seatbelts." This was quickly done. "Now then," he continued, "before I put old Rover into action, have you forgotten anything? If so, speak up now, or forever forget what you've forgotten."

Each child searched mind and person and concluded together, "We've got everything Dad."

"Your anorak's...got them...you'll need them up in the Highlands."

Each child held his/her anorak up for inspection.

"Fine."

Alan Maitland's bellicose manner belied the true feelings he had for his children. He loved them dearly and worked long and hard at his bread and cake route to provide for their necessities. His inbred Scottish nature however, intimidated him and he was reluctant (as his father before him) to demonstrate the love he deeply felt. It was considered a sign of weakness in Highland men to display their gentler feelings. Agnes knew this and was never alarmed by his harsh, disciplinary words.

"Mum," he asked turning to his wife...."did you think to pack them a lunch for the trip?"

"Och," she exclaimed. "I did, and forgot and left them sitting on the kitchen sink. I'll be back in a wink." Out the car she bolted, running up the three stone steps that led to the green painted front door, fumbling all the while in her grey purse for the latch key. She soon emerged carrying three shoe boxes she'd set aside to accommodate the lunches. In her middle thirties Agnes still maintained a trim figure for her 5'4" frame. Her red hair was only slightly dulling with a little touch of grey.

Returning to the car, she deposited a lunch box on each lap, examining at the same time her "creations" as she was fond of calling her bairns. Jamie, the oldest was a wiry 5'6" lad going on 15; with auburn hair and grayish blue eyes that looked out intelligently from their sockets. He was a studious no nonsense boy. Many were the times she'd thanked her Maker for not sending her a lad like some she knew of. Alison, her wee lamb was going on 13 and a carbon copy of Agnes, with reddish blond hair and blue eyes and freckles enough to give away (which she'd gladly have done). She was reminded as she looked at her lass of the need to get Alison's front teeth straightened. An orthodontist was so dear, but somehow, she promised herself, they'd get her teeth taken care of "Perhaps in the Spring." Alison stood 5'2", was particular in her choice of friends, and was in no apparent hurry to grow up too fast. Another blessing Agnes and Alan were constantly thankful for.

Her eyes tried to make contact with Peter; but he was having none of it. He stubbornly kept his head down, seemingly aware of her anxious eyes upon him. "He's angry with me," she sighed. "He's miserable and wants to make sure I am too." Her youngest wain was a small 5 ft. edition of his father. His well built frame was balanced on stocky legs. His brown hair, forever hanging in his eyes, matched the brown of his eyes until angry, and then the eyes became as black as coal. He was a moody child which kept his popularity at a see-saw level. His friends kept their distance when he was in one of his unpredictable moods. Agnes's concern for his unhappiness diminished when she realized that Jamie and Alison now flanking Peter in the backseat, would be taking over where she was leaving off. She consoled herself. She deposited the self guilt to the back of her mind and would not bring it out again until it demanded attention.

"Now," remarked Alan, interrupting her musings, "let's have no talking on the way to the train station. This is the busiest time of the morning and most of the drivers are driving with their eyes half open. It's a good thing they've trained their cars to take them to work without mishap. It's a good thing the cars have more directional sense than their owners."

Agnes pursed her lips in aggravation at her husband's remarks about other drivers, in front of her bairns. "I could give him a lengthy lecture on his own deficiencies as a driver," she thought, but wisely kept still.

After twenty-five minutes of stop and go, near misses and a hair-raising thrill when the car went around a corner on two wheels, the exhausted Rover brought the Maitland family to the entrance of Queen's Street Station. Grinding on the brake drums, the journey was over, to the relief of all passengers.

"You take Alison and Peter. Jamie and I'll follow with the luggage after we park; that is if we can find a parking spot with all this traffic," Alan muttered.

Disheartened by her husband's parting remarks, Agnes took her two children down the ramp which was teeming with excited holiday makers. Children ran hither and yon, screeching at the top of lungs. Parents were feverishly attempting to control with threats of disaster. "You'll be picked up and carried off by the boogie man if you dinna stand by mither's side." Their warnings were cast off as casually as other warnings given from time to time by anxious parents. Disaster was anathema to children on holidays.

In a shorter time than expected, father and son rejoined the family. Having purchased their tickets the previous week, the necessity of standing in the long, long ticket cue was avoided. Waving their tickets high and triumphantly at the gateman, he waved them through. Alan searched for track #5 where the train to Inverness (according to the arrival and departure board) was standing. Quickly threading his family down the long platform toward the middle track #5, he murmured. "Mum, you stay here. I'll get the bairns settled in their seats and join you in a jif."

Agnes knew he hated to see her cry and was sparing her the tearful good-by. She hugged each child, and watched as they crossed the track, go up the wooden step and into a coach. Father and children proceeded through one coach after another until they came to two vacant seats facing each other "this will do nicely." He and Jamie put the luggage in the rack above their seats. "Now, look out the window and watch Mum and me. We'll be on the platform 'til your train leaves"

Taking an oversized handkerchief Alan proceeded to wipe the seats before letting his children sit down. The seats, the size of the back seat in their Rover were stained. The original pattern was hidden by food marks left behind by careless and hungry travelers. Finding no loose dirt, he shook hands with his sons, hugged Alison and bolted out of the coach. They watched as he crossed the tracks to stand beside their mum who had caught up with their coach. Their parents stood waving off and on until a train sidled in between them and track #5.

Agnes, disconcerted at being blocked from viewing the children said morosely; "Suppose there's a train wreck, Alan. We'd never forgive ourselves for sending them. Suppose Peter had some kind of premonition about this trip. Eh?"

"And suppose the sky falls down," replied her husband equably. "Now, look Henny Penny, give it up. It's only for a week. You'll be hugging and scolding them and wishing they were some place else in a week's time."

Peter in angry vexation over the train that had sandwiched itself between him and his parents, almost stuck out his tongue at a small child who was looking at him from the window of the intrusive train. The child smiled and raised her hand in a timid wave to Peter. He gritted his teeth, mustered up a strained smile and returned the wave. His spirit shot upward. He felt good. Now he waved more enthusiastically, surprised that an effort of friendship could change his mood so quickly. He remembered his mum's oft repeated remark. "It's never wrong to do right." Mum was smart.

Passengers were filling the surrounding seats, lifting luggage high above heads. Conversations floated around without any thought of privacy. Peter, momentarily divorced from his mood, watched and listened to the scenes and actions developing around him. "Some kids make awful nuisances of themselves," he muttered inwardly as children ran up and down the coach aisle bumping into passengers entering the train.

His attention focused on a little girl sitting across the aisle snubbing in her tears. Her mother had hugged her, patted her head, and had since left the train. An older girl "I'll bet she's her sister" he mused, was attempting to comfort the child. "She's feeling afraid just like me," he thought and found comfort in a shared anxiety. Peter watched as the little girl adjusted her emotions and began waving enthusiastically at the mother figure standing on the platform. The other train had since departed.

The Maitland children resumed waving at their mum and dad until the conductor shouted "All aboard." He picked up the wooden steps outside the coaches, swung into the last coach, and the journey to Inverness began.

Agnes and Alan Maitland receded into the background, getting smaller and smaller as the train gathered up speed.

The trip lasted six hours. Houses, fields, cattle, cars, and trees hurried past as the train took on the miles like a carrier pigeon delivering its message posthaste. Peter grew tired of watching the countryside fly pass. Alison's "Ooh's, Aah's and did you see that Peter," failed to keep his interest. He turned to the passengers; they were more fun to watch than the outside scenery.

Feeling hungry enough to break a self-imposed fast he'd determined at the trip's beginning, he sampled a ham and cheese sandwich from his lunch box. He glanced surreptitiously at Jamie and Alison to see whether they were noticing his capitulation to hunger. They were, however, engrossed in paperbacks, munching away on apples. A teen lad wearing an oversized white and blue apron pushed a cart down the aisle. "Apples, sandwiches, candy, chips, cold drinks," he shouted. He stopped at seats where money was waving at him.

The Maitlands bought cold drinks. Alison, milk; Jamie, orange soda; Peter strawberry soda. It tasted not too bad with his ham and cheese. He munched away contentedly forgetting his reluctance to be there. The children resisted spending any more money on food. They remembered their dad's admonition. "Don't spend it all on food' as he gave them each a 5 pound note. "If you do, you'll have nothing to show for your vacation but a pimply face."

Peter, restless and tired of watching the passengers and listening to half-heard conversations wished he'd brought a paperback to read. He reflected that his stubbornness to come had only rebounded to his own hurt.

Gazing out the window, the clickety, clickety, clack of the train wheels turning on the rails reached down to his limbs. He began to sag. His eyes grew heavy. Reaching for his red anorak, he lay down with his feet toward the aisle. Jamie and Alison, fully aware of his actions smiled knowingly at each other. In what seemed like a minute in time he was being shaken by

Alison who whispered, "Next stop is ours, Peter. Next stop is Inverness."

Stretching his short body, he disentangled himself from the seat, picked up and shook his anorak, and sleepily looked around. Passengers on all sides were stretching to get bags and parcels and assorted luggage from overhead racks. Alison and Jamie had their cases poised on the table between their seats.

"Have a good sleep, old chap?" grinned Jamie. "I guess so," was the reluctant reply. Alison and Jamie were showing such excitement that Peter for a moment allowed himself the luxury of feeling like a holiday maker.

The train glided slowly into the brightly lit station like a snake making sure of its surroundings. "Inverness, Inverness Station...all out for Inverness," called out the conductor. "With all those signs on the station walls" thought Peter sarcastically, "it seems an unnecessary call."

The train came to a cautious halt. The aisle now was filled with anxious passengers clutching bags, suitcases, and parcels of every assortment. Every person seemed intent on being the first to disembark. The long line positioned itself in front of the children's seats, blocking them in. They waited, luggage on table, until the end of the line passed them. Then they took their place in the aisle. The Maitland children were the last to emerge from their coach. The platform was crowded with people carrying their assorted luggage and treasures. Children were clutching their mothers' skirts without the admonition to "stay by mither."

As they entered the station, Jamie motioned them over to the octagonal information center positioned in the very middle of the station. "Let's stand over there." Alison and Peter were only too glad to follow any leadership even that of their older sibling and obeyed without comment. Scarcely were their cases down on the tiled floor when their names were called. "Jamie, Alison, Peter."

Coming toward them with arms outstretched was an older edition of their father and a short, chubby woman with grey hair, a round face, and smiling blue eyes. Uncle Sam and Auntie Mary. They were hugged, kissed, and slapped fondly on the back. Peter disdained any kissing (except from his mother) and he bit his lower lip in vexation. Their white-haired uncle cleared his throat. This reminded the children of a similar action used by their father when he was warding off an onslaught of emotional feelings.

"Well noo, let's get a good look at ye. My, oh my, ye've grown up. Look at them mither, aren't they a sight for sore eyes?".... "Och" returned his wife 'they're the bonniest bairns in all of Scotland and I'd a known them as Maitlands anywhere in the world even though it's been five years since we laid eyes on them. Noo, let's get oot of here, Sam, and get the wains to the car. They're sure to be tired and hungry and wantin' their tea after that long ride."

Peter for a moment felt ashamed of his reluctance to come seeing how pleased and excited his aunt and uncle were. He was touched by his uncle's hidden emotions. He felt repentant but it soon passed.

With Uncle Sam leading they threaded their way out of the glass doors of the station. Each child carried suitcase and anorak. Sam led them down the street for a block and stopped at an old gray Austin 1100 with a dented right fender and a roof slowly losing its paint. Opening the boot, the cases were deposited. The boot closed and the children soon were settled in the backseat; an uncomplaining Peter ensconced in the middle.

It was raining and with the sky overcast, little could be seen of the town of Inverness. At the bottom of the main street they crossed a small bridge. "That wee body of water we're crossin' is the River Ness," informed Uncle Sam.

Jamie strained his neck to look at the water. He was disappointed and remarked, "It sure doesn't seem like much of a river to me; it doesn't half live up to its reputation."

Sam Maitland laughed heartily. "Och this is only the beginning of the famous Ness. It's a wee river here, but it threads its way doon and aroon 'til it empties into the loch."

"The famous Loch Ness?" asked Alison.

"Och aye" interjected her aunt. "And that's a sight you're not soon to forget."

Alison began a barrage of questions Jamie was too embarrassed to ask, among them, "Is that where the monster Nessie lives?"

Her aunt's jolly laugh was pleasant to hear. "I see, hen, ye have heard of the wee monster what lives in oor waters."

Peter looked disgustedly at his sister for bringing up the subject he'd long ago dismissed as a fairy tale. He caught Alison's eye with body language he knew she'd understand; hiked his shoulders around in disgust and turned his attention to the window.

Alison caught and dismissed his contempt and plunged on with her questions. "Uncle Sam, do you believe there's a beastie in the loch?"

Sam Maitland pulled at his long nose, rubbed his grey stubbled chin and slowly replied. "Well, noo, I've no seen it meself ye ken, but I widny dispute my friends that claim they've met up with Nessie while fishin'. So, I couldny say for certain one way or the other could I, if there is or isny a beastie livin' in oor loch. Ye know there are times when ye have to take someone's word for a thing, especially if ye know their word is trustworthy," he added virtuously.

"Aye," he went on, "there's the Clansman's Hotel doon the road from Drumnadrochit, and several folk were eatin' their dinner and lookin' oot at the loch. Well, sir, up came Nessie's head straight oot of the water into the air and the folk watched her 'til their dinner got cold. I'll tell ye what, they're true believers.

17

O' course their dinners were wasted, but even those canny Scots thought the sighting fair exchange for a ruined meal." He chuckled.

Aunt Mary with a nod of her head added, "I've no seen Nessie meself, but many a tourist's come to oor door asking if I'd seen her with us being so close to the loch. At first I'd chat a wee bit with them, but they became such a nuisance that now I politely say 'no' and gently close me front door."

"How close are you to the loch," asked Alison undaunted that she was the only one asking questions and getting answers.

"Well, hen, we're close enough. I'd say we're aboot a quarter a mile from the embankment. Ye can look doon the bank and see the loch. Some places the bank is high and some places you can walk right doon a wee slope to the loch and go fishin'."

There was little conversation the remainder of the journey; each engrossed in personal thoughts. Forty minutes or so from leaving the station, the Austin was driven around the fence of a small stone cottage bearing the name DREAM COTTAGE on a board hanging over the entrance. Under the title was printed 'The Maitlands' in old English script. Sam Maitland deposited his passengers at the backdoor and put the car in the open shed.

"We'll just go through the back-way," said their auntie; "although it's against my good manners and principles to bring company in through the kitchen.

But seein' we're here and the luggage an' all, ye'll have to overlook my bad company manners this time."

No one made a reply not feeling one was expected.

Mary Maitland opened her black purse, extracted a latch key, inserted it into the lock and they were soon walking into the kitchen. It was a pleasant sight with a welcoming smell. Peter was impressed with the homey feeling. A cobblestone fireplace filled one wall. A large table was carefully laid with plates, glasses, and cutlery to accommodate five people. It was indeed a welcome sight. They were weary. They were hungry. Peter felt a tinge of conscience because of the ill feelings he'd harbored toward the kinfolk who were showing such eager and kind hospitality.

"Well, noo, I'll be showin' you yer rooms and where the loo is, so you can wash up before you eat." Talking all the while she led them up a small flight of stairs into a long hallway brandishing three bedrooms, and the loo planted conveniently between the rooms. Taking Jamie and Peter to the room in the back, their aunt showed them a closet and a dresser with two empty drawers. "You can put your clothes in these, and your anoraks in the closet," she informed them.

The room held twin beds covered with patchwork quilts with a white pillow at each head. The hardwood floor was partly covered with a large rag rug. A gas heater in one corner was to accommodate in cold weather. Peter felt at home; a sign he was taking on additional family ties?   He promptly rejected the notion.

Alison's room had a single bed The room had warmth; the bed covered with a patchwork quilt in browns and yellows. The hardwood floor sported a rag rug made from the same colors as the quilt. "Oh, I love this room. "Did you make this quilt?"

"Och aye, lassie; I like to keep busy. I made the rug you're standing on too. I canna stand bein' idle. The good Book tells us that idle hands are the devil's work tools. I just try to stay ahead of the old devil so he can't get any more tools from Mary Maitland." She laughed her infectious laugh turned around and descended the stairs. "We'll eat oor dinner when ye all get doon." she remarked over her shoulders.

When Alison finally came down looking scrubbed and shiny the five Maitlands sat around the table looking at each other as if for the first time. Uncle Sam smiled sneakily; bowed his head and commenced to say the grace. "For what we're aboot to eat, Oh Lord, we give thanks to you, Amen."

"Sam," his wife scolded, "you forgot to thank the guid Lord for bringing the bairns here safely…

"Och," he responded, "I've been asking Him that all day. There's no use over doin' it." He laughed heartily; he knew his wife disparaged any sign of irreverence, and he often said things to provoke her righteous soul. He laughed again at his "wee aside."

The food was a typical Scottish tea. Raisin scones, currant jam, cold ham, and freshly baked oatcakes. Auntie Mary asked if they'd like tea. Alison replied she would. Jamie and Peter settled for milk. "Well," said Auntie Mary, "It seems at last I've a wee lass to take a cup o' tea with." She laughed. Her infectious laugh blended with the atmosphere of contentment.

Table talk consisted of questions and answers posed by the elder Maitlands: the children's "mither," and "faither," and how they were. Questions were asked and answered concerning their schools; what levels they were in. Their likes and dislikes of sports, and anything else that came to the minds of their elder kinfolk; starved for information from 'hame.' Time slipped quickly away.

It was nearly 9:30 when Auntie Mary suggested that it was time "that ye were away to yer "wee beds." The children were only too glad to oblige and went up the stairs looking forward to a good night's sleep. They were not disappointed. They slept like the dead.

The sun was shining determinately through the bedroom window and playing havoc on his eyelids until it got Peter's attention. He woke reluctantly. For a moment he forgot where he was. Remembering, he turned to say something to Jamie; Jamie's bed was empty. He was gone; so were the clothes he'd worn along with his shoes. Getting up he hurried to the loo. After washing and brushing his teeth he returned to his room to dress. He glanced in at the open door of Alison's room. It was empty; her bed neatly made. Her yesterday's clothes no where in sight.

Hurrying back to his room he struggled into his clothes. Forgetting to change socks and underwear, he made a beeline downstairs. Auntie Mary, tea cup in hand, was munching on a piece of toast, while Uncle Sam was rocking in his chair by the fireplace. Coffee cup resting on the stone hearth, he was half-hidden behind his morning paper.

"Mornin' luv," said his aunt, looking up as he descended the stairs.

"Mornin' lad. Have a good rest did ye?' asked Uncle Sam.

"Morning Aunt Mary; morning Uncle Sam. Yes, I slept fine. Where's Jamie and Alison?"

"Och, aren't they still in their wee beds?" asked Sam with a twinkle in his eye.

"Don't be pullin' the laddie's leg Sam," scolded his aunt seeing the distressed look on Peter's face. "They left the hoose over an hour ago to visit the Loch Ness Investigation Bureau's exhibits on Nessie."

"Oh," murmured Peter a little disappointed at being left behind.

"Sit doon, and I'll bring ye some breakfast," said his aunt putting down her tea cup and rising as she spoke.

Peter sat down to the bowl of porridge (which he usually declined) added brown sugar and cream placed before him. "We've already blessed the food so you can dig right in," his uncle stated.

Peter began eating with reluctance but after a few tastes his mouth accepted the thick, smooth porridge with enjoyment. He finished his breakfast with the satisfaction of fullness.

"Where's the place Jamie and Alison went to?" he asked.

"It's in Drumnadrochit," Sam replied.

"How far from here?"

"Och, only a couple miles away, I'd say," added his aunt.

"Have you been there?" was Peter's next question.

"Aye," nodded Sam, "It's very interesting. They're always addin' new fangled things to look at; new discoveries they call them. There's photos and films of what's supposed to be Nessie taken by folk what have seen her. Scientists blether on about their scientific break- through, pros and cons about the beastie. There's also a tape cassette ye can buy and have a wee look see at all the stuff they've come up with to date on Nessie. Och, aye it's quite impressive. If ye go in the Bureau a believer, ye come oot a more convinced one. If ye go in an unbeliever, ye just might come oot disputin' the so-called evidence with a wee bit more vigor."

"How did you come out?"

Uncle Sam took his time but finally said, "Well ye know lad I dinna ken. I do know folk who have all their wits aboot them who swear up and doon that they saw the beastie. I have to keep an open mind aboot what I've seen at the Bureau" he added virtuously, looking sideways at his wife.

"Mm," nodded Peter.

"How's about a wee bit O' fishin' eh laddie?"

"I'd really like that."

"Well noo, when you've finished wi yer food, come 'round the back and I'll be ready with the poles and baits."

"Right on" exclaimed Peter. Gulping down the last of his milk he sprinted up the stairs; changed into older trousers and shoes (these suggestions from his aunt). He was as excited as he'd been in a long while. "Fishing...wow wait 'til the lads hear about my holidays. I can say I went fishing for the monster in the loch. Even if I don't believe in it." He grinned mischievously. Wonder what I'd do if I really caught 'ol' Nessie?" He laughed and went downstairs.

Peter found Uncle Sam at the shed in the back waiting with poles and bait. They walked toward the edge of the embankment, a good quarter of a mile from the back door. It was a beautiful morning; the sun shining bright above them; the birds singing; the breeze gently blowing warm and soft against their cheeks. Peter felt a contentment he'd not felt before. He was experiencing a bond between himself and this older edition of his father. He would have had a hard time explaining his feelings should he have been questioned. Luckily he wasn't.

They stood looking down the bank at the loch. It was a peaceful scene. The trees lining both sides of the loch were sparse in some spots, thick in others. From where they stood they could see ripples on the water. A few small fishing boats were out in the loch sitting still, patiently waiting for fish to nibble; no one anticipating trouble from Nessie. "Could there really be something to the tales about a monster lurking in the largest volume of water in any of Great Britain's lochs?" Peter mused to himself.

"How deep is the Ness?"

"Well, noo, said Sam, "I'll give ye an example. "If the Americans could bring over their Empire State Building and stand it up in the loch, the waters would hide it completely."

"Wow," exclaimed Peter, whose class last term had compared building sizes for an arithmetic problem.

"Och, aye," continued Sam; "It's supposed to be anywhere from 754 feet to 900 feet plus; it's deep alright."

"How long is it?"

"Well, noo, I've no walked it meself, but it's supposed to be 23 miles long and 1 1/2 miles wide. I didny swim across it neither; I can guess by lookin' at it and readin' aboot it in books." He laughed at himself.

"It sure doesn't look very clear," was Peter's remark.

"Nah, it isny; It's filled with peat that comes doon from the mountains;, little pieces of dirt and grass; makes it difficult to see doon into the water even a few inches from its surface. The divers who have gone doon in their rubber suits have come up half scared out o' their wits for they couldny even see their hands afore their faces. Same way with a wee submarine some book company sent here sometime ago; the peat made it impossible to get a glimpse of anything of importance. However, they keep coming up with new fangled technology for exploring the bottom of Ness. They're bound and determined to find the loch's secret. If there is one."

"What would a big monster live on down there?" asked Peter.

"Och, laddie, there's enough salmon, perch, eel, chard and other fish doon there to feed a whole household of Nessies. That's the scientists' newest argument, that there's enough food doon there to feed an army of monsters. Och, aye, Loch Ness is teeming wi' fish."

"Are we the only daft people that believe in Nessie, Uncle Sam?"

Uncle Sam laughed so hard that he had to wipe his eyes and blow his great nose, before answering.

Peter saw his father's face in his uncle's and a tinge of homesickness swept over him. His joy of the morning was dulled, he felt sad. He missed his mum and dad.

Sam went on. "No, Peter, folk from all over the world traipse up here all year 'round to get a glimpse of Nessie. The Japanese had a big cage ready to launch into the loch some years ago. That's when the British Parliament gave Nessie full-blown recognition and protection. So it seems if those hard-headed, blue-nosed Englishmen took notice and were afraid the Japanese would take off wi' Nessie, that there had to be something to the tale of the monster. I believe they called it something like Nessatoria; or some fool name. However, it made it easier on us wee folk to believe in it too."

"What's she supposed to be?" went on Peter, getting back into the mood of the morning.

"Well, noo, some think she's a sea cow. Some say an overgrown otter. She's been called a sea elephant (whatever that is) or a big eel. Others have called her a large grey seal; some say she's a left over zepplin shot down in World War I. Then, she's said to be a red deer swimmin'; or some rottin' vegetation filled wi' gas. Even some swear she's a poltergeist. Then of course there's them that think she's the invention of the Scottish Tourist Board to drum up tourism."

"Mm," nodded Peter. "But what do you think it is?"

Sam deliberated before answering. "Well, I've no real thoughts, lad. I never was good at scientific stuff, so my opinions come from hearin' the smart folk talk. Some o' my friends plumb for her being a Plesiosaurus."

Seeing Peter's quizzical look, Sam laughed and went on to explain. "Aye, lad, I had to look that one up in the dictionary to ken what the smart folk were talkin' aboot. It seems it's some kind o' reptile what's been extinct for millions of years. I dinny ken. I know very little about what was around millions of years ago; if something was." Sam shook his head in wonderment.

"How come there's such an interest in the beastie now?" was Peter's next question.

"Och, there's been talk aboot a monster in the loch since 564 A.D when that fella Columba shooed the beastie away from a fisherman. But since the 1930's the interest has deepened with the opening of a new road... the one that runs past oor hoose, A82. Well, laddie, it seems that a Dr. Wilson stopped by the loch and up came this beastie, head and all straight out of the water. Well, being a clever chap, he ran for his camera and snapped a picture. Well when it was developed and the newspapers got ahold of it; the monster fever took off like a kite."

"Ye see, 'til the new road opened the loch was hidden by trees and thick brush. When the Wilson photo came out (1934) folk came forward admitting they'd seen somethin' unusual in the loch but were scared to say anythin' ; feared they'd be put away for hallucinatin' or somethin.' No one likes to be thought daft, but from the 1930's 'til now, there've been over

3,000 men, women and bairns what has sworn to have seen her. And some folk have admitted seein' Nessie on land. One couple comin' home near dusk, were scared oot o' their wits when a large, lumbering animal crossed the highway not ten feet from their car. If yer really interested in "Nessie" go to yer library and get a book written by a woman who interviewed folk who'd seen the beastie walkin' on land. I think her name is White, but ye'd better ask yer auntie for the spellin' I'm no good at rememberin' names.

"Mm, how big is Nessie supposed to be?"

Sam Maitland threw up his hand in surrender. "Laddie, methinks ye should take a wee hike to the Investigation Bureau and have a wee look see. I'm a thinkind' ye're more interested in the monster than what ye let Jamie and Alison know."

Peter blushed at his uncle's insight.

Sam took pity on him and answered his question. "Peter, some say the beastie has a small wee head on a long neck; a broad body with humps, four stocky flipper like feet, and a long tail with a rounded end. It's supposed to from 30 to 50 feet long. It's color is anywhere from black to grey, and has wee antennas pokin' from its head. But remember, I'm only sayin' what ithers say, no havin' seen it meself.

"However a group of school children walkin' along the bank saw Nessie, and their smart teacher had them draw what they saw. Would ye believe it, some had more humps than others, but they all pretty much drew the same lookin' beastie. I'll grant wee folk have imaginations, but too many o' them had the same kind o' drawin' for it to be a coincident."

"Sounds to me like you really believe in the monster," teased Peter.

Sam threw his big head back and laughed uproariously. "Let's say I'm just reservin' judgment and keeping my options open to change."

"Mm, I like to see what I'm believing in, so I guess I'll do the same 'til I know more," stated Peter, and feeling very grown up by his stand.

Sam pointed to a path leading down to the edge of the loch. It was not steep, and there was a rocky foot of shore at the end. For half an hour uncle and nephew baited hooks and watched the little red bobbins dancing in the water. Each entertained thoughts of seeing something spectacular emerge from the murky loch.

A disappearing red bobbin, and a tug on Peter's line brought them out of private reveries. "Lad, ye've snared somethin'; slacken yer line a wee bit. Now reel her in; now slacken a bit. Now reel in". Peter tongue between teeth and biting hard followed Sam's advice 'til he took out of the water a large silvery grey fish. Sam put a large net out into the water to catch the fish before it could wriggle off the hook. Into the net went a large fish.

"Och, my, oh my just look at what ye've caught. Would ye just look at that. Yer old auntie is goin' to give you a fair sized hug for catchin' oor dinner. Are ye sure ye're not a seasoned fisherman and been hidin' the fact?"

Peter blushed with pleasure and embarrassment. "No, honestly this is my first real fishing. It sure is a big one, eh?"

"Aye, lad, that it is. Ye won't have to stretch the truth aboot its size. Let's go home. The guid Lord has provided oor meal this day and we dinn'y want to be greedy and clean oot the loch." He laught heartily at the thought of such impossibility.

They climbed up to the embankment, carefully carrying the fish basket, poles and bait. They were as excited as two little boys; age making no difference in their exuberance. They were anxious to show off their catch.

Jamie and Alison were entering the backdoor just as Peter and Sam approached. They were in an excited frame of mind. "Peter, you missed so much by not coming. We saw so many pictures and live film about Nessie." Alison babbled on until Peter taking the large fish out of the basket held it up in front of her. "Peter, you didn't really catch that, did you?" demanded Jamie. "What a fish."

"Oh, aye lad, he caught it all by hisself." Sam proudly announced.

"Oh, my I can just hear you bragging about the whale you caught when you get back to school," commented Jamie, but not enviously. He was sincerely pleased to see his brother enjoying himself. It made life easier for them all.

Aunt Mary "oohd" and "aahd" over the fish. Taking it in hand she went up and down its body assessing its weight. She turned it back to her husband. "Awa' wi ye now, clean it proper, and I'll fix ye the best fish and chip dinner ye've had all year." Uncle Sam shaking his head at her order, went out to do the chore, complaining;. "Such a dictator that wife oh mine has turned oot to be."

"Come with us to the Loch Ness Bureau in the morning" begged Jamie. "You need to see what's there so you can talk about the monster when you get home. After all, there's no use of being up here where it lives and not get acquainted."

"Mm," said Peter intent on dampening their enthusiasm because his fishing accomplishment had been put in the background. "I'll think about it, later."

According to previous agreement, the children rested a while in their rooms after lunch. Uncle Sam had promised them a trip to Inverness after he'd had his "wee afternoon nap." At two o'clock the old gray Austin 1100 was on its way to Inverness, leaving Auntie Mary home to wash her windies "A clean windi, is an informed wee housewife," she stated as they drove off. She said this in jest, but like her countrywomen, Mary Maitland thought it an abomination to have dirty windows in her house.

"I'll let ye wander off by yerselves," Sam started. "I've business of my own in the bank. I've bills to pay or they'll be puttin' me in the jug." He laughed at that unlikely event. "I'll meet ye back at the car in aboot an hour an' a half. That should give ye plenty of time to browse and shop unless ye've got mare money than me to spend."

The car was parked down a block from the train station and the children left their uncle going in the direction of the bank. He'd given them hints about shopping. "The stores here are awfully dear. We've so many Nessie tourists that the merchants take advantage of us toon folk. If ye hav'ny too much money to spend ye might drap by the thrift store down the street. It's called Oxfam. They sell new and old things and handmade things from people that live in other lands. The money collected is returned to their country to help feed and cloth the poor, dig wells, an' just a whole lot of beneficial things."

He pointed in the direction of the Oxfam, took his leave after reminding them to "watch the time, noo, and dinn'y be late in comin' back or we'll just go off and leave ye." Again he chuckled and walked off.

Inverness is not a large town and the children found it to be a friendly one. The folk on the streets were talking and laughing with one another; the shopkeepers were eager to help the children make selections by answering their questions. The Maitlands found it difficult to buy gifts for their parents, for the prices were steeper than they'd anticipated. After hunting through one store after another for bargains Alison suggested they try the Oxfam. Jamie was reluctant at first for he wanted something new to give. Peter straight out said "I'm not going into any rubbish store."

Alison stated she was going anyway and she'd meet them down the street after shopping. She walked away, red braid bouncing down her back. Peter and Jamie looked sheepishly at each other, shrugged their shoulders and followed her.

The Oxfam was not a large shop. Racks of clothes met them as they entered. Sticky tape gave the prices of articles in the store. Rows of shoes. "They look like they're ready for the midden," muttered Peter, lined one part of the back wall. Eventually Jamie found a shelf filled with paperbacks and hardbacks.   Here he parked; here was his heaven; Jamie was a bookworm.

Peter angled his way through other customers and looked into a glass display case filled with odds and ends of dishes and jewelry. A little blue flowered plate caught his eye. Asking if he could see it, the lady behind the counter opened the back of the case took out the dish and handed it over to him. It had a name on the back and a place to put wire through for wall hanging. Knowing his mother's taste for blue flowers, he felt sure this would please her. He bought it.

Alison meandered over to him while the lady was wrapping the plate. Catching a glimpse of it she said, "Peter, Mum will love that."

"Mm" said Peter smiling, "That's what I thought. Did you come up with anything, Alison?"

"You wouldn't believe my find. I bought some beads lying in a cup on the counter. The lady said they were genuine coral beads; just needed to be strung. They cost me a pound. She said they'd cost ten times that much if they were strung and in a jewelry store. I'm so excited. Don't let me forget to get some bead string before we go home." Alison was pleased with her purchase and made no attempt to hide it.

Jamie, still with the books, looked up when they approached. "I've found a great horticulture book for Dad. I just know he hasn't this one, 'cause I know all his garden books. It's almost new. What do you think?" he inquired of his siblings.

"That's fine, but we need to buy him something else 'cause w've bought two things for Mum," practical Alison pointed out. The three children scoured the store intent on buying something else for Dad. Jamie came up with a dark blue paisley tie. "How about this?" he asked. Alison inspected the tie critically. Finding little wrong with it save perhaps a good ironing, she agreed that it was worth the seventy-five pence it cost. Their total purchases came to two pounds thirty-five pence. By dividing the cost by three the children still had some money left. Jamie bought two paperbacks before leaving Oxfam.

Peter jolted them into buying their next purchases. "We haven't bought anything for Auntie Mary or Uncle Sam." Again they searched Oxfam. Peter found a brass trivet with the painting of a house on its top side. It looked like DREAM COTTAGE. His selection was accepted by the others. He was pleased when they said "Great find, Peter."

It was Jamie who found the wooden deer. The carving was twelve inches in height and carved from solid maple; highly polished. At the deer's feet nested a little doe. It was a good buy for eighty-five pence. "The lady said if it were new it would go for eight pounds." They left the store greatly contented with their 'finds' wrapped up in newspaper and resting in second hand brown paper bags.

Peter felt extremely good for he'd made a decision about something his brother and sister had approved of. He felt a bit wiser and older for the experience.

With almost three quarters of an hour before meeting Uncle Sam, they wandered down the street looking into the shops. Tartans as different as their clans, made into scarves, hats, skirts, trousers, gloves and the like, beckoned them from window displays. The plaids appealed to their Scottish nature, but not to their lean pockets.

"Let's see if we can find a tea shop and have a bite to eat," Alison suggested. This seemed a good idea. Crossing the street they saw a small shop with baked goods in the window. Looking in they saw tables occupied by other shoppers. The Maitlands entered. It was a larger shop than the outside indicated. Booths hugged the walls on both sides of the room and little tables sat in the center. The pastry counter had assortments of cakes, scones, and sandwiches. A coffee and tea urn sat on the far side of the counter.

Alison chose a snowball (a round cake the size of a ball, cut in two with jam in the middle, covered with icing and dipped in coconut), and a cup of tea. Jamie chose a salmon sandwich and a small carton of milk. Peter, after much demurring, ordered the same as Alison, but with a small carton of milk. The food was enjoyable, atmosphere congenial, and the accommodations comfortable. This was their first meal alone since coming to Inverness, and it was a pleasant repast.

"You know," remarked Jamie, "I wouldn't have missed this holiday for anything."

Alison added, "I'm going to miss Auntie Mary and Uncle Sam when we go home. I didn't really know what to expect from them before we came. They've sure been good to us."

Peter made no comment. He was still reluctant to give them the satisfaction that he was enjoying himself. However, remembering the large fish he'd caught that morning, brought an unwarranted smile to his face. Alison and Jamie took note of it. A smile from their moody brother was all the answer they needed.

"Mm," said Peter, but his "mm" went unnoticed.

Watching the clock, the children went to find Uncle Sam's car. They left a tip for the unseen waitress, and left the shop feeling like liberal tourists.

"I've got to find stout string to thread the coral beads I got Mum," remembered Alison. One more stop, purchase made, and they were hurrying to where they'd been instructed to meet Uncle Sam.

Their uncle was standing staring down the street. A broad smile filled his face when he saw them coming. He noted their assortment of odd paper bags. "I see ye found yer auntie's Oxfam store," he chuckled as he opened the door of the Austin. "Ye are in fact true Scots by the looks of ye with your purchases."

The journey home was accompanied by the rustle of bags as the children re-examined their "finds." Their purchases looked better away from the store. They were as excited as if they'd shopped at Harrods in London.

Auntie Mary "Oohd," and "Aahd"at their bargains. She was visibly touched at their gift of the trivet "Och, it looks just like oor wee hoose," she exclaimed.

"Let me wash it up a little," said Alison. Taking the trivet she doused it in the soapy water her aunt had been using for washing glasses. The newly washed trivet took on new grace and elegance.

While their aunt protested that they shouldn't have spent their money on them, Uncle Sam sat looking at the wooden deer Jamie had handed him. "Mm, that's a nice bit of carving. Thank ye very, very much," he said, putting the deer on the mantle. The children beamed with the satisfaction one gets from doing something that pleases and is appreciated by the one receiving

The table was set for dinner Alison filled the water glasses and made the tea. She was quite proficient at making tea by now. Her aunt's "Remember, lass, in order to make a guid cup o' tea, the water must be boilin'." She remembered; she was looking forward to making a cup of tea for her mum when she got home.

The main course that evening was Peter's salmon. Never had salmon (or for that fact, any fish) tasted so fresh, juicy and delicious. Peter savored all the compliments that emerged from half full mouths. "Mm, this is so good." He felt good. He'd been the supplier of the meal for his family.

Supper over, table cleared and dishes washed, the entire family sat around the telly watching the six o'clock news. The crime statistics were punctuated with Uncle Sam's outbursts. Aunt Mary chided him to be quiet so they could hear the broadcasts.

Alison brought out her beads and thread and with her aunt's help, they sorted the different sizes and strung the beads into a necklace that looked very professional.

Peter, picking up his anorak, headed for the front door. "I'm going out to stretch my legs," he stated. "Just a wee walk down the road."

"Dinny go too far, laddie, the sun will be settin' in aboot an 'oor and darkness draps doon awfully fast," warned Sam.

"I'll only be gone a wee bit. I won't go too far from the house." Peter, once outside, relaxed. Tensions had been building inside him since dinner. The need to be alone had overpowered him. He had to sort out the turmoil going within; he was enjoying himself too much. He was feeling guilty about not missing his mum and dad as much as he'd expected to do. "I wonder if other changes in life are as easy as this one? I wonder if you ever go back and be what you were before; like erasing things as if they'd never happened. I love Mum and Dad but I love Auntie Mary and Uncle Sam. Will I be short-changing Mum and Dad. I know now that I can exist in another place for a while at least, and this makes me happy and sad at the same time. What's gotten into me anyway?" Peter was maturing at a fast pace, and having a difficult time keeping abreast of his growing up feelings.

Before he could head back to Dream Cottage, he heard a loud rustling noise and saw the tall trees and shrubs moving, although there was no evidence of any strong wind. Something was making an impression on the trees and bushes. "I hope it isn't a two-legged animal with a gun," he silently murmured. The rustling continued and now the ground shook perceptibly. Peter stood motionless. From the top of the trees appeared a small head with two antennas protruding from it. Peter watched as the head rose higher revealing a long, slender neck, peering over the trees. Slowly the head and neck ventured into the open space dragging a large ungainly body. The feet looked like stumpy fins. This was not the end of the apparition. On the wake of the body, came a long tail with a rounded end.

Peter's involuntary action caused him to move backwards. Losing his balance, he landed on his bottom. Directing his eyes upward he watched the enormous animal from a sitting position. "Nessie," he whispered. "I'm seeing the Loch Ness Monster." The monster turned at the sound of Peter's fall, and was stretching it's neck in the direction of Peter.. It was then that Peter saw a little black and white sheep in the beastie's mouth. Peter was about 8 feet away. The monster deliberated, looking in the direction of Peter. Peter held his breath; he didn't want to join the sheep. He heard the pitiful bleating of the sheep; its "Baa, baa," sounded so sad. It apparently annoyed the monster who shook its head and the wee sheep was quiet, the wee bell Peter heard, silent. The monster moved slowly but steadily in the direction of the embankment. At the embankment the animal paused then slipped noiselessly into the loch. A dazed and bewildered Peter sat still until he felt safe. Adrenalin coursing through him, Peter ran as fast as he could following the departing tail. Peter reaching the edge, saw only huge ripples and foam in the recently disturbed loch.

Digesting the events and coming to a sane conclusion, Peter in Scottish vernacular yelled...."I can'ny believe it....I canna believe it. I've seen the beastie. I've just noo seen oor Nessie. I canna believe it." He whooped and hollered all the way to the cottage. "Jamie, Alison, Uncle Sam, Auntie Mary....I've just seen Nessie. I've just noo seen the beastie."

His screams brought the Maitlands out of the house. Uncle Sam yelled. "What's wrong, laddie? Did someone try to harm ye?"

Peter looked at his family standing before him. "You'll not believe me; none of you will," he accused.

"Och', said Auntie Mary, "O' course we'll believe ye, just tell us. We can't make oor minds up if we dinna know what yer talkin' aboot."

Uncle Sam added to his wife's statement. "Come on noo, Peter, what's in your craw? Oot wi' it."

Peter blurted..."I saw Nessie...she walked right in front of me, and I saw all of her. She was carrying a wee black and white sheep in her mouth and the lamb was bleating pitifully. I followed her to the bank of the loch and she slid over and into the water."

Peter stopped. He looked at his family. He saw embarrassment and unbelief plastered on their faces. He lowered his head. "I probably wouldn't have believed Jamie either if he'd said what I just said," he cried.

Uncle Sam moved. Leading Peter into the kitchen he sat him down at the kitchen table. "Gie us time to digest what ye've just said, laddie. Fetch me paper and pencil, Mary. Now draw exactly what ye saw. Go on noo do it right awa' afore yer memory plays tricks on ye."

Renewed excitement gave Peter the ability to draw to the best of his ability the vision running through his mind. The small head, the long neck, the leathery grayish body; the long tail, rounded at the end. He looked critically at his clumsy drawing. Something was missing. "The wee lamb, I forgot about that." He quickly drew the lamb dangling from the monster's mouth. Putting his pencil down he handed the drawing to his uncle.

Sam viewed the drawing critically. There was nothing there that different from Peter's drawing and those he'd seen over the years. "Had Peter let his imagination run away with him," he asked silently. He knew the boy was visibly upset and highly strung out. He took action. "Show us where ye saw Nessie, Peter."

The sun had set but light from the full moon was shining brightly when the Maitlands, flashlights in hands left the cottage. They followed Peter down Highway A82 to a small hillside covered with deep brush and trees. Peter searched diligently for the right spot. Finally he shouted. "Here it is; here's where I saw the monster looking out from the trees."

Uncle Sam's large flashlight searched the area. A definite path was leveled in the brush as far as their eyes could see in the lowering dusk. Something had made a tremendous impression; something huge and heavy. "Aye, somethin's been here alright. Look at that wee saplin' its bent double. Only other thing coulda been a lorrie passing doon that way; but that disny make sense. There's no tire tracks."

Jamie, Alison and Aunt Mary stood staring at evidence that played havoc with their unbelief. Peter became more confident by the visible evidence of his sighting. "Look," he said. "Here's where I sat down in fright." Sure enough a small depression was still evident.

"Jamie," called his uncle. "Run back to the shed and find a bit of Auntie Mary's clothes line and bring it here. Jamie was off before his uncle had stopped talking and was back before he'd finished.

Sam strung the rope across the area of the depressed path, tying it from one tree to another. Satisfied, he commanded, "Let's get oot o' here."

****

Once inside the house, Sam Maitland dialed the 'Inverness Chronicle.' "I know it's a wee bit late to be askin' this, but are there any guid crack reporters still hangin' round the office. If so I've a grand story for him.

"Well," he said in answer to some questions, "What I've to say is up-to-date news of very, very great importance. If yer best reporter isn'y there call him and have him come right over." More exchange between parties took place and Uncle Sam said.. "If ye din'ny think it worth yer while, I've got a good friend who works for the Highland Post, and can get a hold of him."

More exchange, then; "Ye will, well fine. I'll wait no longer than an hour before callin' somebody else. Leavin' Inverness ye can find oor hoose on A82, aboot two miles from Drumnadrochit. White cottage alone on the side of the loch; called Dream Cottage. Ye canna miss it. Now don't be a disappointing me, or ye'll be the sorriest newspaper this side o' the Atlantic. Guid by."

After hanging up he informed his family that a reporter would be right over. "Mary, best make a fresh pot o' tea. This is goin' to be a long night. Things will never be the same for ye again, Peter. That is if they believe yer story."

Peter felt a cold shiver go up his spine. He'd convinced his own people; would outsiders believe him? And if not? Even he could not answer that question.

Uncle Sam put on the porch light and waited by the window pulling the curtains back and peering out. Auntie Mary put the kettle on. Took additional cups down from the cupboard; put digestive biscuits on a plate, Alison sat still, thinking. Jamie sat still smiling. Peter went upstairs to freshen up at his Auntie's suggestion.

It was almost an hour from phoning that a car drove up to the front door. Sam was on the porch waiting when the driver got out of the car.

"Alex Hamilton" stated a 6'2 long leg of a man; copper hair and a cool, no nonsense air about him. Shaking his hand, Sam insisted, "Come in; come in. We've had quite an excitin' time here the night. Let me introduce myself and wife. We're Sam and Mary Maitland; these fine bairns are oor nephews and niece from Glasgow up here on a visit."

"Oh, no," thought Alex Hamilton; "surely I wasn't pulled away from my telly to meet visitors from Glasgow; surely not." After acknowledging the folk in the room, he got down to business. "Now, what is this great story you called the paper about?"

"I'm going to let my nephew tell you; it's his story. Go ahead Peter, tell the man," ordered his uncle.

Peter flushed and timid, had a hard time finding a beginning. "Go on son," urged Auntie Mary. "Tell it just like ye told us."

Alex waited patiently but his ears were not ready for the tale that poured out of Peter's mouth. The boy described the animal known as Nessie others had given at a sighting. He was a little inclined to believe Peter had visited the Loch Ness Investigation Bureau, had memorized Nessie's pictures and had come up with a story bound to bring attention.

He looked at the picture of Nessie drawn by Peter.

"You say it crossed in front of you?"

"Yes, sir."

"Did it make any noise?"

"No, only the noise it made coming through the trees and bushes."

"Any other thing you can think of that is different from the pictures you saw at the Investigation Bureau?" he quietly asked.

"I've not been to the Investigation Bureau," objected Peter. "Only Jamie and Alison's been there."

"Perhaps they showed you pictures of the monster and you just thought you saw it," suggested Alex; trying to give Peter a way out.

"You don't believe me," murmured Peter looking down at his white knuckles fidgeting in his lap.

"It's not that I don't believe you, lad; it's just that I do need a wee bit more proof. You've no idea the number of folk that call us to let us know they'd seen Nessie. When we track them down we find they're only after a bit of publicity. It can get very tiresome running down folk's imaginary sightings. So Peter, you can understand why I am skeptical. Eh?"

Peter nodded and then added, "I did hear a little noise coming from the sheep."

"The sheep?"

`"Yes, the wee black and white sheep the monster had in its mouth. It was bleating so pitifully." Peter shook his head in sympathetic remembrance.

Alex looked closer at Peter's drawing.

"Can you show me where you saw the beastie?"

"Yes."

"Then let's go and have a wee look see."

All five Maitlands, flashlights in hand led Alex Hamilton to the place where Sam had roped off

Nessie's destructive walk.   The area still showed the matted down shrubs and trees; all of recent vintage. This devastated area sent a signal to Hamilton that this was not just a young lad's idea of getting attention. Something had passed that way.   "Could it have been a lorry, he mused. A herd of cattle?"   He walked up as far as he deemed necessary to confirm that something of great weight and length had very, very recently made its imprint on bushes and trees.

"Show me where it went, Peter."

Peter and the others led him along the path where the monster had dragged its body. A definite trail of dirt, broken shrubs, and a depressed embankment, showed that something had made its way to the loch, stopped on the bank before slithering into the water.

Alex stood looking at the evidence. He turned and asked "Mr. Maitland may I use you phone, sir."

"Certainly."

Back to the house they traipsed with Alex Hamilton immediately phoning the newsroom.   "Send me a photographer.   I prefer you'd send Scott McNeill." Conversation, then, "Well, get him. He'll be glad of this picture; it could even make him famous. Tell him to spare no time in getting here. Tell him it's more interesting than that dull telly he's probably watching." He gave directions to the Maitland's cottage.

After hanging up Alex solemnly turned to Peter. "Laddie, the whole of Scotland is going to envy you when the news of this gets out. You'll be deluged with offers to appear on talk shows. Don't let it go to your young head though, because skeptics will ride along with believers wherever your story is told. You'll need a level head and thick skin."

The photographer Scott McNeill made his entrance carrying camera, lights, and other tools of his trade. "What's all this about. It'd better be good for I left a fairly decent mystery to come on the double." McNeill was a 6' well built red head in his late twenties.. He had a small mustache and the makings of a bristly red beard. He sounded gruff, but was an intelligent and dedicated photographer. Many of his shots had made headlines.

Alex pointed to Peter. "Scott, meet the lad who met Nessie crossing the road in front of him."

"Away wi' ye". In Scottish idiom he expressed unbelief "Ye'll no be pullin' me leg will ye?"

"Not this time. Here's the picture the lad drew; but wait 'til you see the actual spot of our Nessie's latest debut."

Once more the Maitlands (with the exception of Aunt Mary who stayed behind to clear away the tea things) with Scott McNeill and Alex Hamilton visited the spot where the sighting had occurred.

Scott, without dialogue, took picture after picture walking along the wide, flattened path made by Nessie on her terrestrial walk. Pictures were taken from every angle; the path to the loch; the depressed ground on the embankment where the monster had descended.

"Well, I'll say this," he mused. "Something awfully heavy walked on this planet tonight."

Gathering his camera and equipment he departed. "I want to develop these. In case they're not what I want, please leave that rope in place. I'll be back first thing in the morning to take additional pictures anyway. Incidentally, when this hits the papers, and it will, you folk had best be prepared for informal visits from Mr. and Mrs. Public. Have fun."

As an afterthought, he turned to Peter and said dryly; "You may be sorry laddie that Nessie chose to walk in front of you instead of some other bloke before this all dies down." Away he went carrying his camera and equipment.

Alex Hamilton left shortly after. He had in mind the notion of putting out a bulletin asking if any farmer had missed a sheep that night. If so, what color. This could make the best copy he'd had in years. He'd have to buy the lass at the station a box of sweeties for insisting that he come out to interview the Maitlands. Such was life.

Sam put through a call to Glasgow as soon as the men had left. He talked at length with his brother, Alan. He heard Agnes in the background asking questions. Alan was answering his wife and talking to Sam at the same time. Peter was called to talk with his father. He answered the same questions that had been put to his uncle. Those near the phone could hear Alan exclaim. "This is no joke, then?"

"No Dad," exclaimed Peter. "I really saw what I told you."

Sam took the receiver in hand. "Alan we're no pullin' yer leg. It's no joke."

"But on the land," objected Alan. "That's a wee bit much to swallow."

"Och, it isn'y the first time the beastie's roamed on land. Get yerself a copy o' a book by some woman named Constance Whyte lots of sightings of Nessie walkin' on land. Here, I'll let ye talk more to Peter."

"Dad." Peter began. But the rest of the conversation was done in Glasgow with Peter intermittently reinforcing his statement that he had "Really and truly seen the monster."

Agnes got on the line. "Peter are you all right, luv? You're not scared or upset?"

"Yes, I'm all right and no, Mum I'm not scared."

"But were you scared, luv, tell Mum."

"Yes, but I couldn't let on I was scared 'cause I didn't want the beastie to come for me. It had such a long, long neck."

"Oh, luv" moaned his mother, "and I wasn't there for you. Let me talk to your Auntie Mary. We'll be talking later and seeing you soon, luv."

Mary Maitland took the phone and the conversation was mostly conducted at the Glasgow end. Mary, however, did get in her observations to Agnes. "He was as white as my new white sheets and shakin' all over. We went to see the very place. No, it's no hoax; Peter did see something. It'll probably be in all the papers up here by the mornin'. Maybe the Glasgow papers will carry it too."

"Oh, dear, that'll mean publicity on this end as well."

"I'm afraid so lass," agreed her sister-in-law. After a few repeated observations, they said good y and hung up.

The phone rang that Friday morning. Sam was already up drinking his morning coffee. "Hello," he said.

"Let me introduce myself to you, sir," said a well modulated voice. "I'm Stephen Chapman from BBC London, Channel 4. We'd like to confirm a fax we received from Inverness that someone in your family encountered"…Here the voice hesitated before using the word; "Nessie?"

" You're correct Mr. Chapman. My wee nephew saw the beastie the other night."

The voice continued. "We'd like to come and bring our television crew to interview him; take pictures of the sighting and of course, interview other members of the family too."

"What time do ye reckon on bein' here?"

"We'll fly into Inverness Airport in three hours," was Chapman's reply.

"That seems like a fair enough warning," retorted Sam. "It'll give us time to clean the hoose and freshen up a bit and put on the kcttle. We didny get much sleep last night. We were all too flummoxed. We'll be ready for ye about 10 this mornin'. And I don't want ye to be hard on the wee lad, he's had quite a scare and he's no over it yet. Ye ken, he's just nine goin' on ten."

"We'll be discreet and handle him carefully," promised Stephen Chapman. After all he had a son of eight and knew what could happen if an interviewer handled a child roughly. He promised complete compliance; said his good by; and hung up.

"Mary," said her husband. "The television folk from London will be up to interview us around 10 this mornin'. Get yerself presentable. I diny want my wife's photo taken in her flannel goon. It could set tongues a waggin'." He laughed uncontrollably.

"Och," said his wife. But she drank the last of her coffee in a hurry; put the cup and saucer in the sink and dashed upstairs. In 20 minutes, dressed, hair combed, with a fresh frock on, she was knocking on Alison's then Jamie's and Peter's door. "Ye'll be wantin' to get up noo...the telly people are comin' up from London to interview Peter and the rest of us celebrities."

Alison was up and in the loo in a flash. Jamie sat up in bed. "The telly people coming here? Wow." He was out of bed grabbing pants, and rummaging in his dresser drawer for his best knit shirt, and clean socks. He shook Peter excitedly. "Up sleepy head; we're, that is, you're going to be on camera this morning."

"What," Peter inquired sleepily. "Did you say something about being on the telly?'

"BBC's crew is on its way to Inverness to interview us; I mean you, about seeing Nessie."

Peter watched Jamie finish his dressing. "You're not joking, are you?" he asked quietly.

"Not on your life; this is for real. You're going to be famous."

When Jamie left the room Peter hurried into the clothes he had worn the night before and made his way to the loo, passing an excited and flushed Alison.

"Oh, I just can't believe this is happening to us" she cried. "It's like a fairy tale. Like being discovered or something." She hurried into her room to complete her fixing up, leaving the loo to Peter.

Peter, hair combed but looking wrinkled, came down the stairs in a hesitant fashion. How did people act when the telly people interviewed them? He came to the breakfast table and sat down to eggs and sausages and toast, his favorite breakfast. He almost began to eat, then stopped. His uncle gave him a nod, indicating that grace had been said. The food, however, didn't taste quite right. He swallowed by telling his throat how to swallow. His system was not on automatic;

he had to dictate commands to his hands, his mouth. "What was going on inside?' he asked himself.

"Don't look so scared son," said Auntie Mary. "We're here for ye. And ye don't have to worry aboot what to say. They'll ask ye the same questions that Mr. Hamilton asked. Ye'll tell them the same as ye telt him."

"But I've never been on the telly before," he whined.

"Well, noo, who in this old hoose has?' was his uncle's sardonic remark. "After all, ye're jumpin' to conclusions that ye're goin' to make the telly; they just might not be impressed wi' ye're sightin'. We're the common folk and no interestin' enough to have ither folk watch us on the telly. So just do yer best and it'll be fine, just watch and see. It may hit the telly and it may hit the floor."

"I would change that wrinkled shirt, though" interrupted his aunt. "It widn'y be right for folk to see my nephew in a dirty lookin' jersey like that. Gang awa' upstairs and find something more decent."

Her firmness brought Peter to the reality of the occasion. He finished breakfast, wiped his mouth, and asked to be excused; then bounded up the stairs. He was getting into the mood of the situation. "Boy, oh boy, what will Timmy Neilson and Phillip Stewart think when they see me on the telly?" He began to project his image to celebrity status. He giggled excitedly.

Coming downstairs looking more presentable, he caught sight of Alison primping in front of the hallway mirror. "I'll bet she and Jamie are going to horn in," he muttered angrily to himself. He entered the front room where his aunt and uncle were busily getting the room in 'company order.'

Peter found that even Aunt Mary irked him in her neat frock; Uncle Sam, trying to look cool irked him; everybody irked him. They were interlopers trying to steal his interview. After all, he was the one who had seen the beastie. He was the one the television folk were coming to talk to. Not them.

A flash back to the train and the little girl waving at him, brought his thinking into focus. He had wanted to stick out his tongue at the child; blaming her for her train blocking his view. He remembered how good he'd felt when he lifted his hand and waved instead. Peter Ellison Maitland blushed. He was ashamed; he was being angry with Jamie, Alison, Aunt Mary and Uncle Sam for presumably standing in his limelight. Intuitively he raised his hand in a wave and his thinking righted itself. They had a perfect right to be part of this limelight. They were his family; they should share.

He smiled at them benevolently. He was ready to face lions.

****

BBC's television crew parked in front of Dream Cottage on A82 at precisely 10:15. One man emerged, the others remained in the truck. Coming to the door, he found it opened before he could knock "I'm Tim Cook from BBC, London" he stated extending his hand to Sam. "Mr. Chapman sent me here to interview the lad, or anyone else who presumably saw Nessie yesterday evening." His indulgent attitude came through loud and clear.

"Well, Mr. Cook," Sam began. "We didny call you, yer station manager called oor hoose for an interview. I take it yer not here oot of curiosity, but rather oot of duty."

Mr. Cook turned an uncomfortable-looking red. "Sorry" he apologized, "but the big brass insisted that I investigate, but I myself am not a believer in the monster theory. Personally I believe it's used to attract tourists to Inverness to bolster the economy."

"Mm, I understand" said Sam dryly. "However, why not listen to wee Peter's tale and then ye'll have more information to act on."

"That's fair," replied Tim Cook.

Peter was introduced by Sam and suggested that before hearing the tale, the telly folk walk to the place of the sighting. This they did.

The walk was filled with apprehension for Peter. "Just suppose the rope is gone and the grass and shrubs are standing up the way they were before the beastie trampled them down. They'll think I'm just seeking publicity." He fretted. His anxieties were wasted for the roped area showed all the same devastation left by Nessie's prowl the night before.

Impressed but not overly excited, Tim Cook turned to his crew and directed his camera men by pointing to specific spots. "Neil, get an angle from this direction. Ian zoom in on the matted bushes, especially those large strong ones. No sign of sheep or cows trampling are there? No. How about lorry tracks. Zoom in on anything that looks unusually suspicious." Ignoring the Maitlands he pointed to the path that led eventually to the embankment. "One of you go down around the edge of the loch and see what you come up with." The crew scoured the area above and below the place where Nessie had slithered into the water.

"Well, so," smiled Tim Cook, "let's go back to the spot where you first saw the beastie and show me just where you sat down."

Peter, surprised at Cook's knowledge of the details, took Cook to the place where he had first seen the monster. Tim Cook surmising what was bothering Peter, laughed. "Alex Hamilton filled me in to the very last detail. I know Hamilton and although I'm not easily persuaded, Alex is a good reliable source for information."

Peter showed Tim the place where he'd backed away in fright; lost his balance and sat down while the monster passed by.

"Tell me about the sheep in its mouth."

"It was black and white, and bleating awfully pitifully," Peter remarked sorrowfully, remembering the wee lamb being carried to its death.

Hamilton had informed Cook that indeed a farmer had lost a sheep the night of the incident. He made a mental note to interview the farmer when he was through with the Maitlands. Tim Cook was a thorough, no nonsense television producer. He guarded his thoughts from those around him.

Returning to the house, the interview took on a more serious approach. Although the atmosphere was charged with apprehension, Peter was made to feel comfortable. The questions were given in a cordial and considerate manner. There was little apparent skepticism in the demeanor of the interviewer. But he wanted just the facts.

Peter went over the same story he had told the newsman and his own folk. It was getting so repetitious that he felt he was rehearsing for a part in a play. The other Maitlands in turn were interviewed, but more out of courtesy. They were thrilled. Alison went pink with excitement; Jamie stammered much to his surprise. His aunt and uncle acted as if they had interviewers in their house every morning at breakfast.

When the television crew left, Aunt Mary went into the kitchen to put on the kettle. "Now, we'll all have a wee cup o' tea and talk."

The suggestion was a welcome respite for the experience had been a taxing one. "There's nothin' like a guid cup o' tea to let relaxing set in," was Auntie Mary's plan of action regardless of the circumstance. It had been a gruesome experience; one they were glad to have had, but not sorry it was over and done with.

In this thinking they were dead wrong.

****

The morning had been a long one; the sun hiding behind the sky of gray. Noon was upon them and Auntie Mary was in the kitchen peeling potatoes for dinner. She was humming tunelessly away. Sam recognized it as her 'thinkin' tune. He was reading his paper, having set it aside when the phone had informed him of the pending visit from BBC people. He noisily turned the pages of the paper causing Mary to look at him.

He looked up as if sensing her gaze. "Nothin' in the paper worth while?" she inquired.

"Nah, I would have thought somethin' aboot oor Peter would have gotten some space in that old rag," he grimaced sourly.

"Och, well, that paper's asleep half the time. Wait 'til the afternoon paper makes its round. Ye'll see they'll have somethin' worthwhile in it," she opined.

Mary's prediction was right; the Inverness Chronicle had quite a spread on the monster sighting; giving it space on its front page afternoon edition. Peter was shown pointing to the place where he'd seen the monster emerge from the trees.

They crowded around looking over their uncle's shoulders (something he normally resented),while he read with feeling every word Alex Hamilton had written. It was a full account of the adventure with

60

Nessie. All the Maitlands were given space with various quotes. Peter's experience was well detailed, but succinct. Hamilton knew how to write.

Dinner at the Maitlands was at 2:30. The table had been set by Alison; water glasses filled by Jamie. Chairs put in place by Peter. The kitchen was alive with muted excitement as they sat down to their steak and kidney pie. The level of excitement was not measured by the number of words attributed to them, but to the importance the quote would have on their friends. They had never been important enough to be quoted about anything. The steak and kidney pie with its mouth watering crust might as well have been kept for another day when palates would have recognized its worth.

The shrill ring of the doorbell brought Sam out of a speech he was delivering (in his mind).

"Who can that be?"

"Well noo Mary, clairvoyance is not one of my better suits," Sam grunted as he got up and went to the front door.

Opening the door he was confronted by a group of folk standing at the door and on the porch and on the steps. Tourists. Tourists who had read of the sighting. People wanting to see the "wee lad who'd had the experience." Tourists who wanted autographs. Tourists who were just too excited to be rational or polite.

Sam Maitland became Sam the diplomat. "Sorry folk, we're at oor dinner."

"We'll be glad to wait," chorused the crowd.

"Suit yerselves, then." He gently shut the door, but not the noise.

Coming back to the table, he and the others tried to go on with their dinner. By now the dinner was getting colder and the folk outside were getting noisier.

"Look Sam, folk are peekin' in oor windies."

"There's some at the back door," shouted Jamie.

"Go right on eatin'" commanded their uncle. "We'll wait them out."

Half an hour later with the table cleared, the dishes in the sink soaking in hot soapy water, the Maitlands went to the front door. Uncle Sam opened it cautiously. Peter stood well behind him. Jamie and Alison and Auntie Mary hovered in the background. Listening.

"Noo folk", began Sam Maitland; "we'll be glad to oblige wi' a few of yer questions. Here's the laddie who saw Nessie. Peter will answer to the best of his ability yer questions for no more than 10 minutes. We're all done in; we've had an uncommonly busy day."

When Peter stepped beside his uncle a murmur of 'ohhhh's' came from the folk on the porch and steps. Then a cacophony of unintelligible words; everyone anxious to have his question addressed. Everyone out shouting his neighbor.

"Whist now," groaned Sam; 'we'll have none o' that. We're decent folk, but I'll withdraw my word about answering questions if ye canny act in a civil manner. Put up yer hands and I'll point to one and Peter will answer yer questions that way. I call that as fair as can be. Agree?"

The combative tone of Sam and his no nonsense stance brought the folk in line. They murmured, "It's fair."

Hands reached to be seen; Sam chose one by one.

The questions tumbled out.

"Where were you when you saw Nessie?"

"Walking along A82 on the opposite our house.

"What did she look like?"

"Small head, little antennas on each side of its head; long, long neck; large grey-black leathery-skinned body; feet that looked like stumpy fins."

"Did it have a tail?"

"Yes, quite a long one."

"Was it noisy?"

"Apart from the noise it made coming through the trees and bushes, no. The only other noise came from the wee sheep."

"Sheep? Where was the sheep?"

"Dangling from the beastie's mouth." Peter stopped for a moment. He was unable to excise the poor wee lamb from his mind as it hung from the monster's mouth.

The folk to their credit commiserated with the plight of the sheep. 'AAAAH' they mourned as they considered the trapped sheep.

"What did the wee sheep look like," persisted a kindly looking mother-figure.

"It was black and white and bleating something pitifully," Peter related. Again a chorus of 'AAHH's' emitted from the people as if wailing on the sheep's behalf.

"When the beastie passed you, where did it go?"

"To the loch. It stopped at the bank before slithering down into the water."

"Did you follow it?"

"Yes."

"Did you see it hit the water?"

"No, I was too far back when it went into the loch."

"When you got there what did you see?"

"A lot of churned water and white froth."

"Do you believe it was Nessie?"

"Yes, I guess so."

A group of teen lads and lassies had joined themselves to the rear of the crowd. They'd been listening to the questions and answers. Snickers and rude remarks floated over the heads of the folk. The people turned around and told them to "Mind yer manners, eh?"

Being thus addressed, they shouted defiantly. "How much did the newspapers pay ye for yer make-believe story? Or was it the Loch Ness Bureau of Investigation what put ye up to it to get mair business from the gullible tourists?"

Uncle Sam drew himself erect, his face taking on an unhealthy red hue, addressed the hecklers. "Awa' wi' ye, ye bletherin' idiots. Go hame to yer mithers perhaps they can teach ye some manners, if ye'r not too far gone from the path of politeness and decency. If ye came for information, ye've got it; if ye came to mock, ye're at the wrang door."

To the rest of the people, he apologized. "I'm sorry folk for the outburst, but we've had a most uncommon experience and we're tired from lack of sleep. So this will end our talk this mornin'. Thanks for yer politeness. Guid mornin'."

"Mary," summoned Sam when they were back in the house, "It's time we got oot o' here or we'll be playing 20 questions for the rest of the day wi' all o' Scotland. Get yer Sunday bonnet on and let's head for

Culloden Moor.. The bairns need a change of scenery and this is the best time to go sight seeing."

Mary Maitland did the unseemly thing; left her dishes soaking in the sink while she went gallivanting in the motor car. But this situation called for redirection of more than her usual household schedule. "We might as well make a picnic oot o' it. Alison, hen, help me fix sandwiches and we'll turn this plague into a blessin'." The two busied themselves in the kitchen and the men folk got the car out and were ready when Auntie Mary and Alison emerged from the backdoor with picnic basket in tow. The mood changed as the car purred down the driveway to the road. It heightened when they saw two cars slowly approaching the front of their house from the opposite direction. "Oh no, more visitors," exclaimed Peter. "Let's get out of here."

"Wave at them bairns and be polite," instructed Mary Maitland. "After all, they're yer public, Peter."

Peter Falls for Nessie

Culloden Moor

Chapter 2

Leaving Dream Cottage was not as easy as expected; cars were driving toward them as Uncle Sam emerged from his driveway. "Wave at the folk luvs" Auntie Mary instructed as they left several cars looking wistfully after them.

"Where are ye headed, Sam," asked Mary?

"Well noo, I felt it aboot time for the wee wains to get a bit o' look at their country's history first hand. How aboot Culloden Moor it's only 5 miles east of Inverness. It'll be a long 'nuff drive. We'll gie to Inverness and then take B-906 right to Culloden. O' course we'll stop in the middle and fill up on what's in that there basket of ye'rs."

Sam's laugh was loud and infectious; holding excitement and relief in its timbre. He would not have had any of his family know the anxiety he held for the children. He knew public minds and spirits; he feared for what a roused and inquiring public was capable of demanding of a wee lad. He gave the car more petrol than usual and sailed down Highway B85 like a young man racing to see his 'sweetie.'

"What's special about Culloden Moor," pestered Alison, interrupting Sam's thoughts.

"Yer no gonna tell me that ye havn'y had that in yer history lessons, lass?" Alison blushed.

Seeing her discomfort, he proceeded in a true Scot's peroration to paint the story of the battle between Prince Charles Edward Stuart (Bonnie Prince Charles) and the British troops at Culloden Moor. "Well, noo, seems like Bonnie Prince Charles on April, 1746 with his 5,000 Jacobites faced 9,000 well armed British troops under the command of the Bonnie Prince's ain distant cousin, General Cumberland. There was such a killin' on the moors. Such awfull unnecessary savagery that old Cumberland was afterwards called Butcher Cumberland. Bonnie Prince Charles' army was no match for Cumberland's for it was poorly organized and ill advised. So its outcome was to be expected; the rebels were wiped out by the well trained Brits and any tag-alongs what joined in wi' Cumberland's trooprs. Aye, it was a sad day for Scotland, 'cause after the free-for-all, legislation was passed forbiddin' us Scots to wear oor own tartans, kilts and other symbols dear to Scots. O' course the Bonnie Prince outsmarted them and got away; but och, 'twas a terrible, terrible .battle."

Nearing Inverness, they spied a decent looking lay-by with a tidy table. Here the Maitlands unwound themselves from the car and were soon seated at the table with Auntie Mary's red and white checkered tablecloth. "We cann'y eat off plain wood," was her remark. "Stick in 'til ye stick oot," urged Sam after saying a 'wee grace'.

Quietness. The sound of birds; the distant lap, lap of Loch Ness was a welcome relief to all. They sat munching and thinking; munching and dreaming until the mood of tranquility was interrupted by Sam's "Well we best be goin." Hurriedly clearing table and replacing uneaten sandwiches in the basket along with the checkered tablecloth, the Maitland clan was on its way.

"We'd best stop at a tourist station, Sam. The children will need to use the facilities."

"Y'er always one step ahead of my mind, Mary. Right ye are."

After their next stop they were soon in Inverness. The direction to Culloden was posted. They were soon on B906 purring along the 5 miles to Culloden Moor. The National Trust for Scotland had restored the moor land to recreate some of the windswept gloom from the site of the last major battle on mainland soil. After walking a bit on the moor, and reading the events with the help of well placed markers, they followed a sign directing them to a tourist shop housing not only souvenirs but a tea room. They gratefully sat down at one of the tables and had their tea.

"Ye ken, that the Highlanders were known as hotheads always lookin' for a fight. So what was the ootcome? Well, sir, they just did awa' with the clans; outlawed them, then and there. They were dismantled forever. But the Scots are a pretty proud race and will have their own way. Di' ye ken the story of a Scotsman named MacNeil? Well sir, the story goes that he was aroon the same time as old Noah was. Well sir, he was asked by Noah if he would like to join him in the ark. According to the wee story, he refused graciously with the words; 'MaNeil has a boat of his own.' Och, aye we Scots are a proud people."

"But I hear people talk about their clan" protested Alison.

"O' course. Ye cann'y outlaw what's in a man's heart. In the nineteenth century Sir Walter Scott's writings (surely ye ken who he is?) well his writings were fannin' the fires o' Scottish nationalism, and oops suddenly tartans, bagpipes, claymores, and heather became ver' popular wi' all Scots. As Bobby Burns would say; 'A man's a man for aw' o' that.'" Ye canna keep a guid man doon. So noo we wear what we want to, and deil tak' the high road."

Animated discussion came to a halt with Auntie Mary's "We'd best be gettin' on hame. The children need to get to their beds early for they have an early rise."

Touring back to Dream Cottage all the Maitlands had something to say about what 'Bonnie Prince Charles' should or should not have done. Discussion about the Butcher Cumberland caused Sam to reluctantly note.

"I hate to tell ye a wee secret but ye really need to ken, that it wasn'y only Brits what fought agin' Bonnie Prince's Jacobites, but some sorry Lowland Scottish men sided wi' the English. Tish, such a pity."

Back at Dream Cottage while their aunt put the kettle on for their supper, the children went upstairs to wash guid and get ready for goin' to their 'wee fleabox' as Sam called their beds.

No one talked much; remembering that this would be the last dinner they'd have as a family for a long time. Merriment absented itself. With the dinner eaten; table cleared; dishes washed, the dreaded 'good nights' were said and the children went up stairs in a solemn mood.

"I'll be up to tuck ye in." promised Mary.

Sam and Mary lingered over their 'cuppa' each engrossed in the privacy of their sorrow.

"Sam it's gonna be awfully lonely withoot the wee bairns. They've come to be such a part o' oor hoosehold." She choked back her tears.

"Whisht, hen, the bairns might hear ye. I know it'll be hard. Seems like they were almost born to us. They're sae much like us in looks and actions. But we'll have them again. Next time, even wee Peter will be anxious to come. Remember how he looked us over at the station. He wasn'y goin' to have any O' us.

He made that perfectly clear. But och Mary when he caught his first fish, he was hooked into oor family for good. Ye ken, the guid Lord knows just how to hook us all."

"I'd best be up and tuck them in. Hope I can keep from greetin'."

"Ye will; after all, ye're a Maitland, aren't ye?"

She gave him a sardonic look. He laughed. She climbed the stairs.

Jamie and Alison were first up and brought down their suitcases. Their aunt and uncle were at the breakfast table; Auntie Mary drinking her tea; Uncle Sam reading his paper and munching on toast. "Guid mornin' lad and lass. Did ye sleep well?" this from Sam. Both agreed that they had. Aunt Mary placed their plates before them; egg, bacon, sausage and fried bread. Milk for Jamie; tea for Alison. They said their own grace and proceeded to eat.

"Where's his nibs?" asked Sam.

"I heard him in the loo" said Alison. "He's probably packing his suitcase."

Aunt Mary went to the stairway. "Peter, ye'd best hurry doon I want ye to have a guid breakfast afore ye start for the train."

There was a muffled "I'll be right down Auntie Mary." Soon Peter descended the stairs slowly, looking at every step and wondering if he'd ever see them again. He dragged his bag down and put it by Jamie's and Alison's.

He took his place at the table and slowly ate the plate of breakfast before him.

The ride to Inverness was more painful for Peter than the first ride from Inverness to Dream Cottage. There was little said and the trip went faster than ever before. Soon Inverness Station loomed ahead. The car was parked; the bags taken out and Auntie Mary's lunch tucked under each arm. Sam gave them each a pound note and remarked. "Dinna spend it a' in one place." He laughed but had to clear his throat as well.

Hugs and more hugs and shy kisses followed. They headed for the platform where the train for Glasgow was standing impatiently to be on its way home.

Katie S. Watson

Chapter 3

They stood there looking lost and diminished as the train snaked slowly out of the station. Jamie, Alison and Peter waved until their aunt and uncle were but small specks on the wooden platform. The children were visibly moved at leaving the relatives they'd known so slightly a week ago but now were the dearest additions to their family they'd not thought possible to experience.

The train picked up speed. The Maitlands tried to erase the week's (especially Nessie) happenings from their minds but without success. A young lad across the aisle whispered to the adult sitting across from him. "Mither," he asked, "Isn't that the wee boy who saw Nessie; the one who's picture is in the paper here?" The woman excamined the proffered paper, looked over at Peter and exclaimed. I believe your're right, son. Why not ask him yourself."

All this conversation had not been lost on Jamie's keen ears.

Stretching his head, the lad addressed Peter and said, "Aren't you that Peter who saw Nessie by the loch?"

Peter gave Jamie a frantic look. Both Jamie and Alison knew he was anxiously seeking their guidance on how to answer. Jamie nodded to Peter who murmured quietly. "Yes."

The lad was not satisfied with just a one syllable answer and rushed on with questions concerning the "Where he'd seen Nessie: what had she looked like; was he scared, and ......" He was ready to increase his non-stop questioning, when Jamie put up his hand and stated. "You have the paper in front of you; all the questions you're asking have already been answered by Peter when he was interviewed. It has been a difficult time for my wee brother and he is truly tired of being questioned."

The woman across the aisle sniffed, "Some people let a little notoriety go to their heads. Leave them alone to bask in their own self indulgent glory." Her statement was unjust and missed the entire mark. Jamie was crushed by her unreasonable assessment of Peter's reluctance. As her own son appeared to be about Peter's age, he felt she should have sympathized with Peter's vulnerability. Jamie smiled negligibly returned to reading his paperback. Peter put his head on his arms resting on the table and attempted to block out the sarcasm.

A teen-lad about Jamie's age, wearing a soiled white and blue apron, came swaying on his feet down the aisle pushing a trolley; shouting "Drinks; chips; candy; cakes,..." As he shouted his wares, hands went up; money waved in his face. He tended jovially to his customers; handing them designated choices; making change and moving down the coach aisle.

Jamie held up his pound note telling Alison and Peter they could settle with him later. He chose an orange soda; Alison milk and Peter decided on strawberry soda. As the lad counted out his change he nearly missed Jamie's outstretched hand for his attention was riveted on Peter. "Aren't you the wee bloke what saw oor monster?" he grinned. "I'll bet a pound note yer the one. Now level wi' me; did you actually see her roamin' in the gloamin' or is it a cooked up publicity stunt to get more folk up Inverness way?' He laughed at his opportunity to say directly to Peter what he and his friends had been making of the sighting...."A lie by a wee bloke to get attention."

The woman across the aisle broke into the conversation. "Oh he's the one alright; but you won't get the time of day out of him. He's become a celebrity and not about to give interviews without a charge." She smirked in the children's direction. Peter turned his body around and became engrossed in the passing scenery. Alison went back to biting her apple with great vigor; Jamie returned to his paperback. Other customers demanded the trolley boy's services forcing him to leave the children's table. He reluctantly left with an insolent smirk on his face. . Jamie however, heard him impart the information that the "wee lad what'd supposed to have seen oor Nessie was in the coach."

More and more necks strained to see them; more and
more voices rose to ask questions. A cacophony of
unintelligible babble greeted the conductor as he
made his rounds. "What's goin' on in this coach?" he
demanded. A dozen voices shouted almost in unison,
" The wee lad what saw oor Nessie is in oor coach!"
The noise continued as questions were shouted in the
children's direction.

The conductor walked the aisle; looking. He came
to where Jamie, Alison and Peter were. He looked the
situation over and seeing the strained, flushed face of
Peter, the anxious looks on Alison's and Jamie's faces;
nodded knowingly at them. He shouted in his loudest
conductory voice. "Whisht, there'll be no more
heckling of this wee lad ye hear? If ye make a nuisance
o' yerselves, I'll move ye to another coach one what's
no so clean; or maybe put ye oot wi' the baggage.. Noo
pay attention to ye'r own business and let them alone
what has other things to think aboott." The thought
of being dislodged from their chosen seats, got the
attention of the loud mouths and they quieted down.

Jamie looked over at Peter's head now resting on
his arms. It was tousled and looked so vulnerable.
"What's going to happen when we get to Glasgow?"
he inwardly groaned. "Would reporters and the telly
camera people be there?. How were mum and dad
taking this. Were they anxious, worried, proud or
totally flummoxed by it all," he wondered.

Jamie a sensitive lad, knew that life, for the
immediate future at least, would not be the same as
it had been a week ago. Should they have dismissed

Peter's claim of the sighting as his imagination and prevented all this fuss? But on the other hand what would that have done to Peter's morale.. He would have been crushed by their disbelief and felt betrayed by his own siblings and kinfolk.

No, no matter what came out of this the truth was always the best way to go. Telling the truth you didn't have to reinvent a story. He knew that he, Jamie would come in for a lot of criticism from his peers when he returned to school in a week's time. How would he face the taunts of disbelief, the name calling of his brother; the reflection that his family gave credence to a lie or a hoax.. Thoughts like a virus of fear invaded his body causing him to shrink from even the thought of arriving at Glasgow's Queen Station. Mum would know what to do and of course so would their dad.

Jamie smiled as he recognized his reliance on 'Mum.' He thought he'd out grown his need for having to rely on his mum to clarify a situation. However his mother's oft repeated saying 'You never go wrong by doing right' comforted Jamie that the support he and Alison had given Peter was 'doing right.' Peter had seen the monster; they had seen evidence; trampled brush and broken trees. They could not castigate Peter for seeing what they wished they could have seen.

This was the conundrum of the unbelievers; the foreseeable hate mongers. Peter had seen what they'd have given their eye teeth to have seen. He had been there at the right time and place; he had taken their spot in the sun. In essence Peter Maitland age nine, had stolen their limelight. This was the thinking of the skeptics even if they were unaware of the origin of their hostility. The moment of discovery had been Peter's, not theirs..

The train with slow surety reached Glasgow without any disruption. There were still glances and whispered snickers thrown their way, but the children kept their eyes averted; on paperbacks or out the window.

"Glasgow, Queen's Station" roared the burly conductor. He made a point of stopping by the children's table and spoke cautiously. "Ye'd be best to let the rest o' this gang oot o' here afore ye get oot yerselves. Gie them time to disburse among their ain folk before ye get off. Guid luck to ye all. Ye'll need plenty o' it." He took a sheet of paper from a pad in his pocket, handed it to Peter and smiled. "I have a wee bairn meself who'd like yer signature." Peter delightedly complied. He felt elated; someone believed his story. The conductor retrieved the signed paper; patted Jamie's shoulder and sauntered down the aisle directing the flow of traffic out the train.

The coach emptied at breakneck speed but to the children each traveler left in slow motion. Without discussed planning Jamie led the way then Peter, with Alison bringing up the rear. Instinctively the older children were protecting their younger sibling. They were finally out of their coach and onto the wooden platform of Queen's Station. They strained their eyes for their parents as they walked the wooden platform. They heard their names called and saw their mum and dad running fast to meet them. In no time at all they were enveloped in the safety net that was mum and dad. How good it felt. Little was said as emotions were too high to deal in the spoken word.. Sobs from their mother could be heard. Their dad kept clearing his throat. "How much like Uncle Sam," Peter reflected; as did Jamie and Alison.

"Let's get out of here right now said Alan Maitland. Walk lively. the car's as close as the bricks of the station. I've been parked here practically all night." Off they hurried up the ramp to the waiting car.

Cameras flashed as they ran up the ramp; more cameras at the top of the ramp; cameras following their every footsteps. "Just one little interview about the sighting from the lad!" pleaded several reporters.

"No comment; the lad's exhausted." Alan Maitland was too burly and too menacing to encourage the reporters to insist too openly. "May we interview him later?"

"No comment."

"Did you really see Nessie?"

Once in the car the children relaxed. They had positioned themselves on the back seat in the same form as when they'd left for Inverness. Agnes noted that there was no fuss about 'seeing out windows.' They were subdued, her 'creations' she noted. "How we've missed you," she said in a voice nearing tears.

"Now mither, don't start yer greetin'.' This is time for action; they're hame. Ye can bring on the sprinkling' system when we've got this mess settled."

Agnes looked balefully at her husband but his sharp tongue dried up the tears welling up in her eyes and choking her voice. "You're so hardened; you couldn't cry if your life depended on waterworks," she sniffed. But down deep she knew he spoke sense. This was not the time to indulge in lamentations; this was a time for action. The television stations and radio talk show hosts had pestered her all day long with requests for interviews. She had been forced to remove the phone from its cradle to get some peace.

A crowd of people stood outside their front gate; camera people were positioned in the front lawn. Reporters with microphones lined their front steps. "Oh, no! how did they find our 'wee hoose?" moaned Agnes.

"You'll not be forgetting our cheery friend the Internet, plus all the other intrusive gadgetry the British public has access to?" Alan's voice was derisive and sarcastic, but it held a modicum of fear. He gave instructions.

"Agnes, get oot yer key" (he ordered in Scot's dialect) "Open the front door. I'll tend to these folk myself."

Agnes fumbled for her latch key, followed her husband's terse directions and was soon plowing her way through the mass of friends, neighbors, reporters and t.v. personnel. With his wife inside the house Alan gave directives. "Alison, hen, you go first; say and do nothing; then Peter oot ye go; same plan as I gave yer mither. Jamie will go after yé and I'll be bringin' up the rear. Remember yer old Dad was once a rugby player."

The instructions were duly followed; the children shutting their ears to pleas for 'Just a wee word'. Soon they were inside their home. Alan stood with his back to the door. Facing the crowd, he lapsed into broad Scots. "Ye'd best bugger off the lot of ye for there'll be no pictures nor confabulations this night. Thank ye very much." He turned and entered the door of his home. He emitted a huge sigh of relief when he closed the door behind him. "The chap that wrote a man's hame is his castle knew what he was talkin aboot," he mused. He grinned impishly in satisfaction at thwarting the gang outside his castle.

"Into the kitchen, your mother will soon have something for you to eat. She's been preparing it all day. There are no windows in the kitchen for the curious to look through.' They traipsed one by one into the kitchen, hung up their anoraks, washed their hands in the kitchen sink and sat down at the set table. It was so good to be home; to smell their mum's cooking. Felt like a year since they'd sat as a family around this table. Cares were forgotten by just being in the security of their parents.

Alison helped her mum bring in the food and drinks to the table.. In no time at all there was such a spread before them that the children were reminded of their first meal in Inverness with Auntie Mary and Uncle Sam.

Sweet and comfortable memories engulfed them when they thought of those loving and caring relatives. Alan Maitland bowed his head for grace; they waited. Soon he was clearing his throat (just like Uncle Sam, thought Peter). The waiting seemed interminably long. Finally Alan said, "Mither, will ye say oor grace the night?" Agnes took over the blessing, "Bless the mercies now before us; help us to eat and drink to thy glory for Christ's sake. And thanks for returning our wee bairns. Amen."

Not much talking went on at the table, but plenty of thinking. Finally Alan began with. "Well, how's my brither and wife? Are they in good health?'

The flood gates opened and Jamie, Alison and Peter all vied for first place to sing the praises of their auntie and uncle. "Oh, Dad, they were so good to us. They couldn't do enough for us. Uncle Sam looked so much like you, only you're younger," were Alison's breathless comments. Jamie added his commendations about Uncle Sam and Auntie Mary. Alan looked at Peter examining his dinner plate. "Well, Peter, what about it? were you bored to death in the Highlands?" Peter blushed a brilliant red and stammered; "Dad I was so ashamed when I met them; they were so very. very kind to us. I could have stayed up there forever, if you and mum had been there too. I went fishing with Uncle Sam and caught the biggest fish I'd ever seen. Even Uncle Sam said he'd not seen its equal.'

Jamie and Alison were quick to add. "Auntie Mary cooked it for our dinner and it was the best tasting fish we'd ever eaten.'

Small talk about their adventures in Inverness; their shopping and the gifts they'd bought. Remembering their presents, the children rushed up stairs to retrieve their precious gifts for their parents. Alan and Agnes looked across the table at each other and smiled. "Remember what it was like getting Peter to go?" Agnes nodded her head. "Seems as if he's grown a peck since we last saw him."

"He'll grow a mile after his privacy is invaded by Mr. and Mrs. Curious Public. He'll be reduced to tears following the accolades. Agnes, I'm real worried about this whole business of Nessie. Do you think he saw the real thing?"

Agnes peered over her tea cup at her frowning husband. "I've no doubt of the validity of Sam and Mary's statements.. Yes, Peter saw the real thing. Have no doubts about it or you will divide our household. We must stick together through this avalanche of media. We cannot give them even an inkling that we are entertaining negative thoughts about the sighting. Whisht now, the bairns are coming down."

Soon Alan and Agnes were exclaiming delights over the presents from their children. The coral beads were a treasure; the blue plate found an immediate place on the wall of her kitchen. Alan's gratitude for his horticultural book and tie was genuine. There was contentment in the Maitland household. It would soon be broken; but their enjoyment of the moment satisfied the longing in their hearts to be together around the kitchen table.

Alan Maitland cleared his throat and addressed the subject he had been dreading. Looking at Peter in particular but including Jamie and Alison in his search for information, asked the question looming up but not discussed....as yet. "Were you alone when you saw the beastie, Peter."

"Yes, dad, I'd gone out for a wee walk after dinner; wanted to think alone about Uncle Sam and Auntie Mary. I was so ashamed of my feelings before meeting them. I felt like I was being pulled in two; liking them so much and feeling I was giving them more thought than you and mum."

'Oh son,' cried Agnes; ' it's alright to love someone outside of dad and me. It's just that the situation presented itself a little sooner than you were ready. It blind-sided you. But it's alright."

"How far from your uncle's house were you when you saw Nessie?"

Alan got back to his subject.

"Not too far, for it didn't take me long to run home and call Uncle Sam and the rest to tell them what I'd seen. Probably about fifteen minutes from "Dream Cottage."

"Then what happened?" persisted Alan, intent on getting details before they faded from Peter's mind.

"Well, like I said I ran and called everyone; they looked at me like I'd lost my mind. But Uncle Sam got flashlights and they followed me to where Nessie had crossed in front of me. He sent Jamie back to get rope and roped off the place that was all trampled down."

Jamie interjected; "Dad, at first we thought Peter was fooling us; but when we went to the place, there was no doubt that something awfully big had trampled down the brush and broken down trees and dragged something toward the loch. No question about it; something had stirred up a mess of the ground. We even saw where it had slithered down into the loch."

Alison, not to be undone interrupted with; "Uncle Sam had Peter draw the beastie. It was just like the pictures Jamie and I had seen when we were in the Loch Ness Investigation Bureau. Only difference, was the wee lamb hanging from the beastie's mouth. Oh, dad, we felt sure that Nessie had walked in front of Peter as he said."

Agnes shook her head and dabbed at her eyes. "You could've been killed by that monster. I had a premonition that something would happen to one of you."

"Now, let's not play prophet after the fact. We have to get all the information while it's fresh and not make any contradictory statements about the event. We'll be giving spiel after spiel until the furror of a 'Nessie sighting by a Glasgow lad' dies down." Alan instructed Peter to describe in detail the size, color, length of the monster and anything else he could remember.

"Well, she was big. Her neck was long with a wee head on top. Looked like she had antennas on each side of the head. Her body was kinda grayish-black. Reminded me of elephantt' skin I've seen in the zoo. The body was real fat like. Then it had a tail that seemed so long in coming out of the bushes. The beastie turned its head toward me when I fell back on my bum. I guess it had keen ears, for I didn't make too much noise. I tell you I was so scared, I could hardly breath."

Agnes emitted a groan.

"How long did it take the beastie to get to the loch? Did it travel fast or slow."

"It kinda moved in slow motion, but at the same time it took very little time to get to the embankment. I really can't say. I was dazed and scared. But it didn't take too long, I reckon."

"After it got to the embankment, you said it stood still for a while?"

"Yes, it seemed to take its time before slithering down the bank. I could still see the wee lamb and I felt so sad for it that I wanted to cry. Then it just disappeared and when I ran to the loch I could see only upset water and a lot of foam on the loch's surface."

"When the newspaper man arrived, did he believe Peter?" This was asked of both Jamie and Alison.

Jamie thought that he didn't. Alison echoed his thinking.

"When did he change his mind?"

"When Uncle Sam showed him the roped off place. He thought it might have been a lorry passing through but he couldn't find any tire tracks."

Alison added..."When he first saw Peter's drawing, he looked like he didn't believe Peter. When Peter talked about the wee sheep in the beastie's mouth, he perked up and asked more questions. Then he called for the photographer. I think by then he was a bit convinced."

"Jamie lad, then what happened."

"Well, Alex Hamilton asked to use the phone, and...."

"Who'se he?" interrupted his mother.

"The newspaper man, Agnes. Go on Jamie"

"Well, he called a chap to hurry and bring his camera to Dream Cottage. He sounded convinced 'cause he said something like 'the man would kick himself if he didn't get this picture.'"

"Go on."

"Auntie Mary gave Mr. Hamilton some tea and he kept on talking to Peter and asking him more questions. He said that when the story hit the papers Peter would be in for a lot of publicity. Wasn't too long before the photograph man drove up and Uncle Sam let him in.. He didn't want any tea from Auntie Mary; he was in a hurry to know the story and take the pictures. Alex Hamilton told him what had happened. Scott (the photograph man) said 'ye'r daft mon; ye'r pullin' me leg, eh?' Then we all went to see the roped off place. Mr. McNeill took pictures right and left."

"Was the ground still pretty much torn up; the trees and shrubs still matted down."

"Yes, Dad, butted in Alison. "I was worried about that very thing but when we got there, the ground and trees and things were just as broken down as when we'd first seen it with Peter."

Alan Maitland was intent on assessing the reactions of the two grown men who would have been of necessity, skeptical of such a story. He was more convinced than ever of the reality of Nessie's walk that night. "Anything else you can think of" he inquired.

They thought. Peter came up with "I heard Alex Hamilton say he was going to put out a bit in the paper asking if any farmer had lost a black and white sheep that night."

"You could tell the color of the sheep?"asked Mum.

"Oh, I'll never forget that. It was so pitiful dangling from the beastie's mouth. Yes, I saw its color; black and white."

"After they'd gone, what happened next?"

"We sat and talked and then went to bed. Uncle Sam said we'd best get sleep for the next day would be a bugger. He was right. Folk began arriving at the house in the afternoon while we were eating dinner. They rang and rang the door bell. Uncle Sam had to tell them we were eating and would talk with them when we finished."

"Then they began looking in the windows," Alison said in a high pitched voice as she remembered the intrusion.

"Uncle Sam went out on the porch with us behind him and talked to the folk. They asked Peter some questions and he answered them. They were pretty decent people. Until some rowdies came along and began -heckling us and Uncle Sam told them to 'bugger off.'"

Alan Maitland smiled knowlingly. He knew his older brother could hold his own in any situation. He was glad he'd been his children's champion.

"We left soon after dinner for Culloden Moor.. Auntie Mary and Alison packed a lunch. We had a grand time driving up into the Highlands. They were so beautiful and peaceful." This from Jamie.

Agnes looked at the kitchen clock. "Goodness it's way past our bedime. Your Dad's got to get up early for work. We'll get back to 'Nessie' tomorrow. Up the stairs the lot of you." She gave each 'bairn' a hug. "I'll be up later to tuck you in." She smiled as they ran up the stairs.

Turning to Alan she spoke seriously. "We have a problem. I've been contacted by Mr. Stephen Chapman of BBC television this morning. He wants to bring cameras to the house or if we don't like that, they'll send cars for us to take us to their studio here in Glasgow. What should I tell him? He's going to get back to me in the morning.]

Alan rubbed his hand over his brow and frowned. "It's no good trying to ignore the media. It's no goin' awa'. When you talk wi' him in the monring make arrangements to pick us up at the hoose... After you talk with them prepare the bairns for their debute on the telly. Now be definite that all the children appear; not just Peter alone. I'll no' have the others slighted."

"I'd best get them some new clothes," mused their mother.

"No, they can go on television in the clothes they wear to Sunday School and the kirk. If their 'claes' are guid enough to meet the Lord at the kirk; they're guid enough to meet any television executive."

Agnes blushed and changed the subject. "What time should I say is convenient? You're the one we have to consider."

"I can probably get Hughie Gilchrist to finish my route. Let's say 2 o'clock for them to pick us up. I don't want that gaggle of folk around the house like this evening."

"Fine. I'll tell Mr. Chapman when he calls."

They turned the lights off and sauntered upstairs. Agnes looked in at her 'creations' and Alan made ready for bed. By ten-thirty the Maitland family was wearily asleep.

Jamie was the first up and out of the house the next morning. Telling his mum he was going to the library, he ate hurriedly and was out and on his bike before Alison and Peter made their appearances at the kitchen table. Jamie reached the public library before it opened. He circled back to the newsstand and bought a paper. Sure enough there were pictures of them getting off the train; pictures of them hurrying to the car; pictures of their home and their dad standing addressing the crowd on their front steps. He had mixed feelings. He felt elated at the newspaper exposure but at the same time had reservations as to the final outcome.. Was the family able to handle something this big without making a fool of itself. He half read the paper and biked to the library.

Standing before the reference librarian, Jamie stammered his request; feeling as if everyone in the library was listening tto hear his choice of books. "Could you please tell me what the call number is for books on monster sightings, especially land sightings of the Loch Ness Monster?" The librarian raised her eyebrows and smiled broadly. "Let's see what we can come up with. Your request is not the first one so perhaps our holdings will be slim pickings. However, if that's the case I can get on-line and request a book from another library. Come with me."

Katie S. Watson

Chapter 4

While Jamie watched the librarian computer search for land sightings of Nessie and followed her to the stacks, Agnes was replacing the phone in its cradle.

Alison and Peter came sleepily downstairs for breakfast. Their mum set breakfast before them in an absentminded fashion. Neither child talked for their thoughts were playing havoc with their intellect. Nothing untoward had entered their world before, they were at sea as to how to cope.

There was no easy way to break it to the children of the coming television interview. "We're to be interviewed by the BBC this afternoon," their mum blurted out.

"This afternoon?" they shouted. "This afternoon! We're being picked up around two o'clock by one of their drivers and driven to the Glasgow studio of BBC. Your father will be getting off work early and we're to be dressed and ready when he comes home."

"What will I wear Mum?" this from Alison. Peter looked at her thinking "They'll be interviewing me, not you." He kept his mouth shut but was aggravated by this intrusion. He had forgotten how to share the limelight. "What will I wear, Mum?" he demanded angrily ; the emphasis being on the "I".

"We'll wear our Sunday clothes. Dad doesn't want us making more out of this than can be helped. Now eat your breakfast and get back up stairs and clean your rooms; and give yourselves a good bath. When Jamie comes home he'll be wanting to use the loo."

Realizing that Jamie was not in the house they asked; "Where's Jamie, Mum?"

"He went out early to bike to the library He didn't tell me what he was going there for. Hope he's not late in coming home; especially today."

"I can bike over and get him," offered Alison.

"We'll see. It's not necessary yet. Later on it might be and then you can go."

In the meantime Jamie was seated at a library table in a more or less secluded spot. Around him were several reference books the librarian had helpfully gotten him. From the material he gleaned the following. There were various land sightings dating from 1527 to the last recorded land sighting in 1963. The sightings were located on the North shore Drumnadrochit ; Inchnacardoch Bay; Invermoriston; Inverfarigaig;Urquhart Bay. etc. The sightings were reported by: school children "Horrifying animal seen moving from swamp area in Unquhart Bay into loch." (1930)

Mrs. Eleanor Price-Hughes (1933) "Large creature emerged from bushes and vanished into loch." Col. L. MCP Fordyce (1933) "Like a cross between large horse and camel with hump on its back. Small head on long neck. Grey in color:" Mr. and Mrs. George Spicer (1933) "Large creature crossed road 140m in front of car. Thick body with long neck. Grey 7.5m long. Moved in a jerky movement then slid into loch."

Jamie noted that more sightings were seen in the 1930's.

Looking at the reason for the multiplicity of sightings he read about the making of a new road along the loch that gave more exposure to Loch Ness by cars and local folk.

The two last sightings in the '60's were: Torquil MacLeod (1960) "Grey/black mass with elephant like trunk. Pair of front paddles in all 13.5m long." L.N.I. (1963) "Seen and filmed on shore 4km away Film no good because of distance but guessed at body of 5m long." (This last was not a land sighting but one in the loch.)

Jamie made note of Internet source for future reference: (http,/www.lochness.co.uk/nessie/sightings/ sightl.html.) Date: 2-21-00.

The various comments by those interrupting the monster's walk were encouraging to Jamie. Peter then, was not the only one to give testimony to the fact that the beastie was also known to walk on terra- firma. It gave him a confidence that he was in sore need of. Jamie knew his interest in Nessie searching was to back up the claim of his younger brother. He knew the questions, the raised eyebrows, the sneers and the coughs of disbelief they all faced when school took up. His intent was to give Alison and Peter information to deal with the snickers of unbelievers; and bolster the faith of the believers.

He jotted down facts pertinent to their 'cause'. He decided to forego detailed information about the legend's beginning. He noted only that in the year 565A.D. the Irish missionary Saint Columba was walking along the edge of the loch and found some local people burying a townsman who had been mauled by the lake monster. The missionary, according to legend came face to face with a very odd-looking beastie, something like a huge frog only it was not a frog. The monster was going after a man in the loch to do him harm. The Saint was supposed to have shouted "Go thou no further nor touch the man. Go back at once."   Legend has it that the monster stared at the missionary then turned itself around and disappeared into the loch. However interesting was this legend, Jamie really wanted facts he could sink his teeth into. He read to find them.

Recorded sightings became more frequent with the new road, A82 . Opening in l933 it gave extensive view of the loch to motorists, locals and tourists alike. The road opened on the northern shore of the loch between Fort William and Inverness. Thousands of sightings have made Nessie an international pet and an extremely important tourist attraction.

The few sightings of Nessie (on land) describe her in general as being about thirty to fifty feet long with an eight-foot neck and a small, flat head. She (many prefer to think of her as feminine) has a long tail and a wide back with one or more humps and elephant-like. Some accounts say her eyes are slits, like a reptile's. Others say she has two tiny protrusions like horns. She has powerful flippers or paddles and can move fast; has acute hearing and appears bashful. She has been seen at all times of the year, mostly in the early morning. One land sighting produced information that the beastie carried a sheep in its mouth. Jamie did a double take when this bit of information crossed his vision. A sheep, just what Peter saw! 'Wow.' Jamie was more excited about this bit of news than many of his recorded statistics. He was more ashamed now of his doubting Thomas stance he'd first taken at Peter's tale.

Jamie sat back in the library chair and unbent. He hadn't realized how tense he'd become while reading about Nessie. "Every thing Peter told us is reinforced by others who had seen her walk. Even about the sheep." He hugged himself with joy and would have shouted out triumphantly if he'd not been confined to the ambience of the library.

His doubts now taken care of, he delved into pertinent facts about the loch itself; why it had evoked so much international interest. After all there were many lochs in Scotland. What made Loch Ness so special. He was surprised to learn that Loch Ness was the second largest loch in Britain. It was also deeper than the oceans that surrounded the United Kingdom. At one point near Urquhart Castle (the place of many Nessie sightings) Loch Ness is twice the mean depth of the North Sea. It was supposedly created during the Ice Age, a product of a huge fault known today as the Great Glen. Loch Ness, the second largest loch in Scotland contains more water than any other lake in Britain; 263,000 million cubic feet of water. It is fed by eight rivers and sixty major streams. The water temperature is forty-two degrees Fahrenheit all year round. The loch is unpolluted but contains particles of peat that wash down from surrounding mountains making visibility below the surface very poor. It is a common saying that Loch Ness never gives up its dead. No bodies are ever retrieved from Loch Ness.

Scoffers have stated the obvious. "Such a huge monster could not survive for long (let alone millions of years) in the loch; not enough food." This fallacy has been put to rest by the many divers and scientific measuring of not only the depth of the loch but also of the abundance of huge eel and chard and countless fish of all sizes and description. Salmon grow to a tremendous length in the loch. This placid loch has a depth of more than 700 feet; deep enough to hide a 42 story building.

Jamie felt rather than saw the librarian as she approached him. He looked up and smiled a bit sheepishly. "Are you finding what you want?" was her question. Jamie replied "Yes, to a certain extent. I would like to have been able to log more land sightings. Wonder why no pictures were ever taken of Nessie as she came out of the loch."

The librarian smiled and stated. "You're one of the Maitland children we're reading about who supposedly saw Nessie?"

Jamie blushed and nodded his head.

"Did your brother take a snap of her?' she asked pointedly.

"No, he didn't."

"Perhaps others who experienced those irregular sightings didn't have a camera or were too addled to reach for one and snap her picture. People don't act rational when the unusual occurs. It's when the situation is over that one asks, 'Why didn't I do this or that?' not while one is experiencing a phenomena at their door. Are you having a difficult time with publicity seekers?"

He shook his head; "I got out of the house before anything happened this morning but last night when we came home we were mobbed by folk and telly people and reporters. My dad had to get rid of them. But I suppose I should be on my way home and see what's happening."

The librarian smiled and added; "My young brother and some of his pals spent three days of their holidays scanning the loch for Nessie."

Jamie was almost afraid to ask her opinion but she volunteered it. "On my brother's watch, he saw nothing. However, the second day one of the many scanners, took a great picture early in the morning. My brother is a firm believer and still sneaks away to do a little Nessie watching. He's hooked."

She addressed the question that hung in the air: "I haven't seen it myself. Yet, I don't dispute those who have actually seen and taken pictures of the beastie. There are thousands of loch sightings by not just the gullible of this world, but by honest and responsible citizens."

Jamie smiled broadly and asked. "Do you ken what time it is?"

"A quarter to the hour of twelve."

"I must be off and see what's going on in my house. May I check these books out; I've not finished with them?"

"Of course, go to the check out desk, they'll take care of you. Good luck to you and your family, you'll need it." She turned and went into her office.

At the desk Jamie put down the books he wanted checked out: "Science Looks at Mysterious Monsters" by Thomas G. Aylesworth; "Of Scottish Ways" by Eve Begley; "Scotland" Fodor's Guidebook; "The Loch Ness Monster" by Ellen Rabinowich; "Around Loch Ness" by Frank Searle; "Beastly Tales" by Malcolm Yorke." He bundled them in his arms and took them to his bike. Placing them carefully in his front basket, he mounted his bike, and went whistling home. As he turned into his street the whistle became a low groan. Parked in front of and across from his house were cars with people gazing out the car windows. Folk were crowded around their gate; some had ventured into the small front yard and even up the steps. Jamie did a double-take and cut through a neighbor's yard and managed to get to the back of his house without being seen. Trying the back door, he found it locked. He knocked and said not too loudly "Mum, let me in it's me, Jamie." The door flew open and he was grabbed and pulled inside by Alison .

"What's going on" he asked unnecessarily.

"What do these folk want?"

"Me" wailed Peter. "They keep calling for the wee lad, that saw the beastie to come out and talk to us."

"Where's Mum?" Jamie asked.

"Upstairs getting ready."

"Ready for what?"

"The television folk are picking us up at 2 o'clock and we're going to be interviewed on television." This news came from an excited Alison. "You'd best go upstairs and wash yourself and get changed into your Sunday School clothes. Mum has our clothes laid out for us and we've already washed up. When she comes down we'll go up and dress."

Jamie stood motionless taking in her words. He turned to Peter and saw his sullen look. "What's the trouble, you not want to be interviewed? Or are you not liking the idea of us being included?"

Peter turned a bright red; nothing got past Jamie. "Of course I want you there. It's just I'm kinda scared that I'll make a fool of myself and the chaps will laugh at me at school." Peter felt better by using this excuse. It got him out of his selfishness and brought him to the realization that he needed Jamie's and Alison's presence as back-ups. "Why did you go to the library?"

"I went to get information on Nessie being seen on land. There's plenty recorded sightings of her in the loch, but I didn't know if anyone else had testified that they'd seen her walking on land."

"What did you find out? "Alison and Peter asked in unison?

"There are several recorded land sightings, but no pictures taken. I talked with the reference librarian and she asked me if you'd taken any pictures. When I said, 'No' she said; 'You see, the incident would be sudden and traumatic and people would think of taking pictures after the event.' She was sure nice; she got me some books and got on the internet for me."

"Jamie. is that you son? Come up and get washed and changed we're going to BBC Station affiliate in Glasgow. Your dad will be home soon and I want him to be able to get dressed without interference from any of you. Peter and Alison I'll be down in a minute then you scamper up and get dressed. I'll look after you hair when you get dressed. Now look sharp, Jamie and get on up here."

"Coming Mum.." Jamie took the stairs two at a time.

Agnes was soon down and Peter and Alison went up the stairs to ready themselves. They dressed hurriedly and were soon back downstairs getting their hair taken care of. Alison's hair was brushed until it shone like a copper braid. Peter's stubborn hair resisted all attempts to make it lie flat and out of his eyes. Agnes looked them over; gave them a pass and went into the kitchen to get tea and sandwiches for Alan.

The doorbell pealed but they ignored its persistent clamor. The bell had rung countless times before. They knew the reason and they ignored its demands in order to concentrate on getting ready for their appearance on the telly. "Mum, someone's at the door; don't you hear the bell?" Jamie's call from upstairs brought peals of laughter from them. "If he only knew," sighed Alison.

"We hear it and are ignoring it. Get dressed and come down and get a sandwich before Dad comes home. Hurry now."

Alan Maitland drove his car to his home and could not get into his driveway; cars and folk blocked it. He brought his fist down angrily on his horn. "Get yer cars oot o' my driveway, or ye'll have a smashed fender." He began to climb on the bumper of one car and the driver quickly backed away from the drive. Alan drove slowly down his drive scattering people who got out of his way. They knew an angry Scotsman when they heard one and Alan Maitland was angry. Getting out of the car he turned to face the frenzied crowd who'd circled his home. "Ye'll get to see wee Peter and his brother and sister this evening on yer BBC telly. We're on oor way noo to be interviewed. Gie us a break and let us get oot of here before we leave Scotland altogether and end oor days in London."

The effect on the crowd was magical. They recognized the joke and the predicament of this family. They backed away, many of them getting into their cars and moving on. Not all. Some lingered across the street for a glimpse of the Maitlands as they came out of their house. The television and radio reporters held their ground. They were used to abuse; they knew a story when they heard one and this was big time. They, kept their distance, but were visible.

At two o'clock a big car drove slowly up to the Maitland's house. The BBC television logo was painted on its sides. The driver got out and made his way up the steps and rang the bell. He waited patiently and when no one answered pressed harder. This time, the window curtain moved and then the door opened to let him in. "Sorry," apologized Agnes, "but we've been pestered all day." The driver smiled understandingly.

At 2:10, the Maitlands one by one left their home, entered the luxury car, and were driven slowly away. Shouts and questions were hurled at them; camera lights followed them to the car. The Maitlands were learning how not to be intimidated. The press's microphones got nary a whisper but the cameras were blessed with many a good picture of Peter, Alison and Jamie as they entered the big car with their mum and dad. The car moved smoothly and unhurried down Glamis Road.

The large car could accommodate six people with ease; not counting the driver's area. Although there was a glass division between passengers and driver, no one spoke. There was tenseness among them; each developing a speech of his/her own. No one knew what to expect and each was expecting that he/she would perform poorly. In less than thirty minutes the driver drew up before a large, impressive stone building. He got out and opened the door for the Maitlands. This was a new experience for them and they shyly said "Thank you." The driver led them into the building through glass doors that opened at approach. He led them to the receptionist's desk; repeated their names; said, "Have fun" and left.

The lady at the desk pecked at her intercom. "The Maitland family is waiting in the lobby, thank you." She smiled and informed them that someone would be with them immediately. No sooner had she spoken than an elevator opened in the middle of the huge hall and an impressive man, almost the size of Alan approached them. Holding out his hand to Alan he stated; "I am Stephen Chapman from BBC, London. I take it you are the father of this remarkably plucky lad?" After Alan had made the acknowledgement, Mr. Chapman shook hands with the others and led them to the elevator. Pressing button four the Maitlands were whisked up to the fourth floor and out into a huge, elaborate studio. This was their first view of the inner workings of television land and they peered without embarrassment at the various sets that made up the studio. One set was familiar to them; the anchor man's desk that they viewed every night when watching the news.

They were soon seated in what looked like a small, well appointed living room. Peter sat beside his mum; Alison and Jamie on a larger couch with their dad. Mr. Chapman seated himself in front of both couches. He began with; "Tim Cook interviewed you in Inverness; he's unable to be here as he is on assignment out of the U.K. I will try to be as careful and considerate of your feelings as he was. I have a small lad of nine myself, and wouldn't want him harassed or embarrassed. Let's discuss before the cameras roll, the gist of this sighting; how you came to be out that evening walking near the loch. Don't feel pressured; just tell it as if you were telling your tale for the first time. Don't embellish or add things that didn't happen. We're only interested in facts not fantasies. Our audience is made up of believers, skeptics; and down right doubters who will ring us up as soon as we're off the air with their comments; good, bad, ugly. Now, Peter tell me in your own words just what happened the night you saw Nessie walk? This is being prerecorded so that should make you a little less nervous. It will be seen after the 6 o'clock news. Now please begin Peter."

Peter relived the night of Nessie; was interrupted many times by Mr. Chapman's questions. This went on for a good thirty minutes until the lights on the studio rose and the camera men began to position themselves for shooting. It was almost time to be 'On the Air.' Each held his/her breath; would they survive this?

The ON signal alerted the Maitlands and they felt extra adrenalin coursing through their bodies. Mr. Chapman sat in his leather armchair as calm as if he were in his living room watching the telly. His 'Good evening' was addressed to the television audience. He then proceeded to inform the public that they had a special treat in store for, "Appearing with me in the studio is Mr. and Mrs. Alan Maitland and family. If you recall just a few days ago, their youngest lad, Peter, actually saw Nessie of Loch Ness cross before him. He will relate his story to us. There are many believers and there are many skeptics as to the authenticity of the notion that there dwells in Loch Ness a monster. Perhaps tonight you will still be a skeptic; but perhaps after hearing 'wee' Peter's description, you just might become a believer. At least you will have some second thoughts. Or you may be left with no opinion at all."

After introducing Alan, Agnes, Jamie and Alison, he turned and addressed Peter. "Now here is Peter, the lad who says he saw Nessie.

"Tell us Peter, how was it that you decided to take a walk by yourself in that lonely part of the loch, and after dark?"

"It was dusk not dark, and I wanted to be alone to sort out some things that were bothering me."

"What could be bothering a lad of nine?"

"Well, you see, I hadn't wanted to go to Inverness and stay with my aunt and uncle. I'd put up such a fuss before leaving Glasgow and practically glowered at my auntie and uncle when I met them in Inverness. Well they'd been so good to me . My Uncle Sam had taken me fishing in the loch and incidentally I caught my first fish and it was a whopping big salmon. Well, all their kindness had gotten to me and I was really ashamed. I went out for a walk to sort out my feelings. This was the first time I'd met anyone outside of my mum and dad that I really cared for and I wasn't sure I was being fair to my mum and dad 'cause I cared for Auntie Mary and Uncle Sam. Feelings were all mixed up inside me. That's what took me out that evening. It was dusk; not yet dark. I walked and it was about fifteen minutes away from the house that I heard the rustle in the trees and felt the ground shake."

"You're quite introspective for a lad of nine."

"I'll be ten next month."

"I see. When you heard the rustle in the trees and felt the ground shake, what thoughts went through your mind?"

"I thought maybe there were hunters about because of deer or maybe a lorry turned off the road that made the ground shake. That's what I first thought. Then I saw something rise above the trees."

"Describe in detail what you saw. Take your time."

"There came out of the trees a small head on a very long neck. It turned left and right and then dragged itself out into the open. That's when I saw its body."

"What did you do? Were you scared?"

"I don't rightly ken if I was scared; I was too flummoxed to know how I felt.

I kinda backed up and tripped and sat down on my bum. That's when its head turned and looked in my direction. I was sitting down looking up at it."

"Can you describe its color and size and general shape?"

"Well, it was real, real long and looked grayish-black. From where I was its skin looked like the skin of an elephant. I can't remember too much about its eyes; but it seemed to have something like horns on each side of its head. I was scared by then for I saw it had a wee sheep in its mouth. The sheep was bleatin' awful like. Then the beastie shook it and I heard a we bell, then the lamb went real limp."

"What did you do next? Did you get up?"

"No, I was too scared. I didn't want to join the wee sheep. I stayed sittin' down 'til the beastie dragged itself to the loch."

"At the loch, what did this monster do?"

"It stood on the edge of the embankment for what seemed like a long time, but was probably only a minute. Then it slithered into the loch."

113

"Were you able to see it in the loch?"

"No, all I saw was a lot of churned water and lots of waves."

"You're next move was what?"

" I ran shouting as loud as I could 'til I got home. Uncle Sam and Auntie Mary and Jamie and Alison ran out to see if I was hurt."

"When you told your tale what was their reaction. Tell us exactly how your news was received."

Peter looked at Jamie and Alison before answering. "I think they thought I was putting them on. I guess I would have thought the same if Jamie or Alison had told me what I'd just told them."

"What were your Uncle Sam's and Aunt Mary's reaction?"

"They got real white in the face. I know they wanted to believe me, but it was something too difficult to believe."

Stephen Chapman was getting more incisive with his questions. "Why do you think they didn't believe you ? When did they change their mind?"

"Well Uncle Sam and I had talked about Nessie. He'd not seen her; Auntie Mary had not seen her and they'd lived a quarter of a mile from the loch for years. Uncle Sam was open minded. He had friends who had seen Nessie and he wouldn't doubt them 'cause he knew them to be truthful people. He told me that

there were things you took by faith if the folk tellin'
you were not daft.   At first they were real skeptical.
Auntie Mary fixed me a cup of tea and Uncle Sam gave
me paper to draw what I'd seen. He was still a bit
skeptical for it looked like pictures Jamie and Alison
had brought from the Loch Ness Investigation Bureau.
I could see he still doubted me. I then remembered the
wee lamb and put it in the beastie's mouth. I think it
was soon after that that he asked me to show them the
place I'd seen the beastie."

"What happened when you got to the place?"

"I was so scared the trees and bushes would be
standing up straight and the trail of the beastie to the
loch be gone. But the trees were bent double and the
bushes smashed and the ground showed something
heavy had been dragged to the loch. Uncle Sam sent
Jamie back to get rope. I forgot to tell you that Uncle
Sam had a grand flashlight that lighted up real good.
Jamie soon came back with Auntie Mary's clothes line
and roped off the place where the beastie had been.
Then we went back home."

"Was the family convinced by now?"

"Well, Uncle Sam got on the phone and called a
newspaper man and convinced him to come out for
'the story of his life.'"

"Did your uncle tell him what the story was?"

"No." He said, "If he didn't come oot he'd be the
sorriest newspaper man this side o' Scotland; and

he would give him just so much time before calling another newspaper. Uncle Sam wasn't foolin' either."

Alan Maitland chuckled softly; he knew Sam's insistence got results. He'd often been the recipient of his brother's determination.

Mr. Chapman smoothly went into the absence of any pictures being taken of Nessie on land by Nessie watchers. "How would you answer that, Peter, if put to you by Nessie watchers?"

Peter thought out the question carefully. He knew that he'd been told of the hundreds of pictures taken of the beastie rising from the loch. A land sighting was not easy to justify for no pictures had ever been taken to verify the fact that Nessie had been seen on land. He responded slowly to the inquiry. "I don't know how to answer that question. I only know what I saw. I wished I'd had a camera with me; but I had no idea that I'd come up against a beastie. I'll probably never get another chance of seeing It walk on land. again."

Here Jamie cleared his throat for attention. Mr. Chapman turned and asked. "Do you have something to contribute here, Jamie?"

"Well, I spent a good few hours in the library this morning looking into 'land sightings' and found several accounts of people who had seen exactly what Peter described he saw. All of those folk failed to get a picture too. They were too amazed, or too addle-brained at the sight of the creature. Only after it was too late did they wish they'd gotten a picture. There are not too many such sightings, but one woman wrote a book about all kinds of 'sightings' and she records sightings on land. I remember the name of her book. 'More than a Legend.'"

Stephen Chapman thanked Jamie for his input and nodded his head in agreement. "Often we think and act after the fact. What trouble we would save ourselves if we acted during the fact."

Addressing his next remarks to Alan, Stephen Chapman asked with extreme caution; "When your brother phoned you and related Peter's experience did you believe him? Is Sam easily persuaded into accepting a phenomenon such as a walking Nessie supposedly seen by a young nine year old? When he went to view the site, was he convinced without a shadow of doubt that the tracks were not made by hunters or a large lorry?"

Alan felt the hairs on the back of his neck bristle. He calmed himself before answering Mr. Chapman. "I ken my brother real well. He's no fool. He'd never jump to conclusions. Was he convinced that Peter had seen the beastie? Unequivocally, yes. I ken it's hard to believe; I still have to remind myself that my wee lad is no liar and my brother's no fool. But to answer your question. Sam was convinced something unnatural took place that night; photographs were taken of the trampled ground. I suggest you take a look and decide for yourself."

Mr. Chapman was mollified. With a few additional remarks to the Maitlands, he ended the interview with these sentiments. " The viewers will make their own judgment as to the authenticity of the Nessie walk seen by Peter Maitland. There will always be those who will not believe the unseen 'til they see the unseen themselves. Others will accept by faith the nine year old's (going on ten as he wants us to remember) account of his first-hand look at the monster of the deep as she crossed his path. Each viewer has the opportunity of exercising his/her faith as they see fit.   Thank you Mr. and Mrs. Maitland, Peter, Jamie and Alison for being our most interesting guests in many an evening. Good night to all." The lights came up as the cameras shut down. It was over. Good bys and handshakes concluded the event.

If the ride to the studio had been quiet, the ride home was somber. No one spoke. The driver glanced at his rear view mirror and saw a deflated family sitting there chewing their insides out. He was not a Nessie believer but he had sympathy for their situation. They came across as decent folk. He had grown up in Glasgow and knew how the winds of sentiment could shift if the public felt it had been conned or seen as fools.

Turning into the street the driver found himself blocked in by cars crowding around the Maitland's house. He whistled in annoyance. "Well folk you still have John Q Public camped at your door. Just wait until your interview comes on the telly tondight, you'll be flooded with phone calls and knocks at your door."

Alan dismissed the driver's remarks with; "Just get as close to the house as you can; we'll take it from there."

"No offense, Mr. Maitland, but I'm responsible for your safety. I'll get you to your front door if I have to climb over these buggers in the road." Saying that he pressed his hand on the horn and started in earnest to plow into the cars blocking the street. His car was bigger and soon the road cleared enough to navigate to the front of the Maitland's house. "Stay in the car 'til I open the door" he ordered. Properly admonished they did as he said and remained seated until the driver opened the door. Agnes had presence of mind to have her key out. Once the door was opened the children went first up the stairs making their way through the crowd; then Agnes and finally Alan Maitland. The driver followed the procession and stopped when they were inside their home. He turned without a word and descended the steps, got into the limo and drove away without one glance at the crowd of gapers.

Agnes went upstairs to change into a housedress and more comfortable shoes. She instructed the children to go to their rooms and change. Alan stood in the kitchen listening to the directives, but completely lost in his own thoughts. "What happened to them in the studio when Peter was telling his story to Stephen Chapman?" Alan became immersed in cold sweat. His son was pouring out his story; but there was disbelief in the room. Chapman had not believed a single word Peter had spoken. Contagious doubt crept over Alan. Could it be possible that Peter had imagined the event?

He was angry with himself for doubting his son. Yet, Peter was impressionable; perhaps he had been reading about the beastie and in his own mind was convinced he had actually seen it. He'd have to get reassurance from Sam. He reached for the phone and put through a call to Inverness.

It was good to hear Sam's 'hello.' After small talk the brothers got down to the business of interviews and the story of Nessie. Alan came to the point. "Sam, when we were interviewed in the BBC Studio this afternoon I know that fellow Chapman didn't believe Peter. My problem, Sam, is that when folk like us get into situations out of our depth we feel inferior to those who are big muck-a-mucks. I felt like crying while the wee lad poured out his experience to someone who politely took it in as middle class rubbish. Not that he said so, but the feeling was there. We're home now and we feel pretty low. We've no said anything to each other, but I reckon we all feel like charlatans. Our house is surrounded with gapers and the phone will probably begin to ring itself hoarse when I get off talkin' wi' you. I guess I'm callin' for a bit of advice and a bit of assurance."

"Well, Alan, I'm ashamed of ye no' believin' yer own wee wain. It isny a hoax.   If ye'd been up here there'd be no doot aboot it; ye'd a' seen fer yersel' the evidence.   No everybody's goin' to believe but if ye dinna believe Peter, that lad's in for a tough time. He'll be left a' by hissel' and somewhere doon the line he'll begin to doot what he saw. It'll happen if ye run for cover.

"Course the big shots dinna wanna believe. They're too intelligent to believe in the guid Lord, Himself let alone a beastie in the l och that thousands of daft folk have seen and taken pictures of. Get back to yer family and let them see yer backbone. They'll all need yer strength, man. Dinna leave them dootin' aboot how ye feel. I'll wanna see the six o'clock news and events. I don't wanna miss yer debut. Talk at ye later."

Alan was cheered and ashamed by his brother's remarks and admonition. He had let the opulence of the studio; the expensive clothes worn by Chapman; his suave way of talking down to the interviewees; while at the same time exuding interest in their information, shake his faith in his own lad. What a dolt he'd been to fall for the impressive trappings that led to disbelief. He shouted up the stairs, 'Where's everybody? Agnes, is there no food in this hoose? I'm starved after that dressing down we got at the studio. We've got about half an hour before we see what fools we made of ourselves on the telly. Anybody hear me?"

Agnes came running down the stairs. She had changed her clothes. She'd been crying. Alan put his arms around her and whispered, "Dinny greet hen, it'll be alright, ye'll see."

"O Alan," she sobbed; "he didn't believe Peter or Jamie either. He looked so smug; I felt like crawling out of there on my hands and knees; felt like we were there just to try to get a wee bit of fame. As if we cared about that. I'm so worried about Peter. He's taking it hard. I was so worried about you. I felt you had your doubts. O Alan, if we don't believe him, who will?" She sobbed louder.

"Whisht, they're on their way down. Dry yer eyes. Put up a good front. The Maitlands have only begun to fight."

Jamie and Alison came into the kitchen to find their mum putting on the kettle and their dad attempting to set the table. Alison took over the task. Alan spoke to them both. "We've been through the ringer tonight. You felt as we did that Chapman didn't believe Peter?"

They nodded. Jamie spoke sullenly. "He thought we were some jerky family after a bit of publicity. He was nice enough, but it came across loud and clear that he felt it was a hoax. Peter's in his room crying. I heard him when we passed his door. I'm glad you and Mum are on his side, and of course Alison and I believe him. I had to fight hard in the studio to remember what it looked like near the loch where the beastie had walked. I began to doubt the story myself. But I wouldn't let myself fool myself."

Alison admitted to the same doubts and had felt exactly as Jamie had described. "Then I got mad. Mr. Chapman hadn't seen what we'd seen yet he was sitting on his high horse judging us as if we were fools."

"When you've fixed us a bite, we'll eat it by the telly. I'm going to have a talk with Peter." Alan made his way up the stairs.

Finding Peter's door locked he gave it a sharp knock. "Peter, open the door." His heart was beating fast as his ears strained to hear movement inside the bedroom. Finally the key turned in the lock and the door opened slowly showing a disheveled Peter still in his Sunday best, trying not to look at his dad. Without saying a word, Alan put his strong arms around his son and drew him close. "Never mind the experts son, they've everything going for them but common sense. We all felt the rejection even though it was served in fancy platitudes and smarmy smiles. We know the truth. It may take some time for it to be proved, but someone or something will turn up to validate your date with Nessie. Now let's go down and have a bite and watch us make fools of ourselves on the telly. First, get out of your Sunday duds." Leaving Peter to change Alan descended the stairs whistling 'The Bluebells of Scotland.' Agnes smiled, her spirits uplifted.. Jamie and Alison glanced at each other and grinned broadly. Dad was in control. Everything was going to be alright.

Peter made his way downstairs just in time to hear BBC's anchor start the 6 o'clock news. A tv table was set for him. Alan Maitland pressed the mute button and said a short grace. Turning up the sound, they sat solemnly eating their snack in front of the telly; not a habit Alan subscribed to. "Dinner time is family time with feet under the table; not stretched out in front of a telly." They listened intently as Mr. Chapman introduced them and watched their reactions as they were addressed. Mr. Chapman looked very self assured and they, to their dismay looked like frightened rabbits. As the interview droned on to conclusion, the family squirmed and changed positions a dozen times.

There was an audible sigh of relief when Mr. Chapman finished with his 'Good Night,' and the program was ended.

Silence washed over the living room like a wet blanket. It was broken by a small snicker, then a little laugh and then uncontrolled laughter. It began with Agnes, picked up by Alan, then Jamie, Alison and last of all by Peter.

Agnes spoke through her laughter. "I looked like a woman sitting at the dentist's waiting to be called in to have all my teeth pulled; Why was I so scared?" Jamie said

"I looked like dumb bunny eager to tell Mr. Maitland something he wasn't going to believe anyway. I'll bet the chaps at school give me a good drubbing."

Alison regretted that her dress looked washed out and wished she'd worn a brighter frock. "Anyway it wouldn't have impressed that man; nothing we could have said or done could have."

Peter who had not laughed so heartily remarked that his cowlick kept creeping up and he looked like he had a feather on top of his head. "I kept my eye on that cowlick all the time I was listening to Mr. Maitland on the telly put me down. I was scared in the studio for half way through I felt he didn't believe me. That's when I really felt bad and wondered if I had dreamed up the whole thing."

Alan remarked somberly. "We've been through a lot today. We're not through with ridicule. It'll come in all packages; smarmy ridicule; hostile ridicule; accusations of being liars; and remarks we've not dreamed of to this day. But we've got our bearings; we've got our faith in the truth. We have each other. These are the strengths we must hold on to. I'll come under fire at work tomorrow. I'm not looking forward to being called a publicity seeker. Regardless, we must bear in mind that we are a unique family. This has happened to the Maitland family; not the Jones; nor the Browns, but to us. So God put the beastie in front of Peter, and we'll have to trust the Almighty to give us the courage to deal with it."

The family was silent once more. Then looked at one another. They smiled and then began to laugh again. "Watch out, the Maitlands are on the warpath against cynicism in high places."

The phone rang. Agnes looked for help. Alan picked up the receiver. "Alan Maitland speaking. Well, thank you very much, I do appreciate those kind words. I'll pass them on to my family, and to Peter, of course. Good night." Putting down the receiver he announced; "One of the viewers called to tell us how much she appreciated our story. She's a firm believer in Nessie. She did say it was news to her that she'd been seen on land. She is going to get the book Jamie recommended, and read it. Let's make a chart and mark the plus and minus remarks from our phone pals."

That evening the phone rang, and rang. After each call a mark was put on the plus or negative side. By bed time an exhausted family made its way up to bed. The phone had mercifully been taken off the cradle. It could not interrupt their sleep. They were in control. This was only the beginning. The second day after the broadcast would bring more than phone calls.

Alan left for work at his usual time 6:15. a.m. He steeled himself against the ribbing he knew he was in for. He was not disappointed. Other drivers filling up their vans were waiting for him and with tongue in cheek asked for his autograph. Followed by, "Did ye bring us Nessie's autograph? When do ye have an audience with Her Majesty ? Alan. surely ye want to share wi' yer buddies all that notoriety."

Alan acknowledged their taunts, answering their questions all the while filling up his van with bread and pastries for his everyday customers. The men had their fling at him with innuendoes but they but they were not vicious chaps. They too began filling their vans for their customers. Work is important to the Scottish man. His dedication to caring for his family gets first priority. The men were good buddies of Alan's and would stick up for him when pushes came to shoves. The subject, although not completely dropped, was set aside as they drove their vans to the various routes.

Agnes was having her second cup of tea after Alan left for work. The children were still asleep, for which she was grateful. Not an early television watcher, she felt the urge to see if any new comments had been given after they'd gone to bed. Sure enough, the early morning newscasters were having their go at interpreting Peter's sighting. Listening to them, Agnes was amazed at the knowledge they spouted about an event they hadn't been privy to. It was easy to see how well dressed, articulate newsmen and women could color the news and convince the uninformed to their way of thinking. "If I weren't Peter's mum" she remarked to herself "I would call Peter a wee liar, just out for a bit of notoriety. So I can understand the folk who call and make fun of us." One newscaster's feeble attempt to give consideration to Peter's story was quickly shot down, as being naïve.

Naïve by a more aggressive reporter. Agnes got tired of their babble and cut off the telly. She took up her Bible and found solace in the 23rd Psalm, her favorite. She sat thinking, then went back to bed for another hour's sleep before the children woke up.

The telephone's insistent clang, clang, woke the family. The children were forbidden by their dad to answer the phone.. Agnes reluctantly came downstairs picked up the phone with "Hello."

"Good morning, am I speaking to Mrs. Maitland?" Agnes replied "Yes."

"Let me introduce myself, I am William Bremner, manager/owner of Radio Clyde, Station l02.5. I watched the BBC telecast last evening, and let me say Mrs. Maitland, your family came across as credible in spite of the short shrift you got from the BBC anchor. I would like to interview Peter and your other children for my radio broadcast and let people call in and ask questions of them. I believe it will help your family deal with the publicity it is certain to get over this monumental event. I can come to your home if you'd be more comfortable in your own surroundings. I am sure you will want to check with your husband before giving me an answer. I can assure you, you will be treated in a less deprecating manner . I will leave my number in order to contact me when you make your decision. I can only urge that you not hesitate too long. This is news now, a few weeks from now it will be off the plate. You have a right to air your story. Time is of the essence."

Agnes listened carefully and was impressed with the sincerity of Bremner. "I'll call you as soon as I talk it over with Alan. Probably after 5 o'clock." Mr. Bremner gave her both his office and home number. They said good by and the conversation was over.

Agnes was setting out cereal and milk as the children came downstairs. They said their grace and had just begun to eat when the doorbell pealed insistently. Agnes motioned for the children to remain seated and went to the door. Five children were at the door asking to see Peter. Agnes recognized some as friends of Peter's. "We've just sat down to breakfast," she informed them.

"Can he come out to play wi' us," asked one of his school chums? Agnes demurred before answering. "Come in for a minute." She led them into the front of the house and told them to wait "'til we're through with breakfast."

Coming back to the kitchen Agnes told Peter his chums were in the front room wanting to see him. He flushed and said; "Oh Mum what am I to say to them?"

"You won't have to say anything. They'll be asking you all sorts of questions and you'll answer them to the best of your ability. That's the least you can do. We can't go into hiding; we've got to face people. We're not liars, so why should we behave like we've done something wrong. Finish eating; go upstairs and dress and then go into the front room and be yourself with your school chums."

This advice was followed. Peter finished eating; went upstairs two at a time wanting to get back to being normal. He wanted to see his friends; play some soccer; go bike riding. Forget about Nessie. This was his intention, but it didn't turn out that way. Before the day was over Peter was immersed in Nessie. Dressed, he entered the front room to find his school chums waiting expectantly for him. When he came in, they stared at him as if they were seeing him for the first time. "Well" said Peter, "what do you want to play; soccer, or go biking?"

Jimmy Thompson spoke up. "We came to find out all about yer experience at the loch. We want to hear it first hand from yer ain mouth, that ye really saw the beastie. Then we might believe ye. Right noo we don't know if yer lying or no."

Peter flushed with irritation, and remembered the talk Alan had given them when they got home from BBC. "Not everyone is going to believe you, but we do; it really happened. Some folk you'll never convince, and some folk will need no convincing for they know you."

Peter looked at his school chums and sighed. Of course they wanted to know what he'd seen; wanted to hear so they could decide for themselves whether or not he was telling a fib. He also knew their motive. They wanted to brag about first hand knowledge of Nessie.He lightened up smiled, and began his story. "I really did see ol' Nessie. She really did walk in front of me."

The questions erupted like Noah's flood. "Oh Petie, what did she look like, really look like?' Jimmy Thompson asked. "I'd have been so scared she'd come after me and eat me up."

"She was big and long and leathery looking," was Peter's response.

"Ye said it was carrying a wee lamb?" Robert Todd was reminding him. " What did the poor wee sheep look like?"

"It was a wee black and white sheep. It was bleating so pitifully it near broke me in twa."

"What do ye think it was gonna do wit' it?" fretted Archie Peebles.

"DInna be a moron Archie" chided Jimmy Thompsonj. " It was gonna eat it. The beastie wasny takin' it doon into the loch to play wi'."

The boys laughed at the thought.

"Ye said on the telly that the beastie got mad and took it oot on the wee sheep" was Bobby White's input.

"That's too true," continued Peter. "When Nessie got to the edge of the loch the lamb wiggled and the beastie gave it a really mad shake and the poor wee thing went limp and didnna even whimper."

"Ye think it was dead then before it went to its watery grave?" asked Alec? That was kinder than being alive in a beastie's mooth. Alec was a sensitive boy; most especially where animals were concerned.

"Well, that last shake was so powerful that I heard the bell around its wee neck tinkle. I hadny thought much about that before," mused Peter. Remembering.

Sitting with tea cup in hand, drinking the black liquid slowly, Agnes smiled as she listened to the excited voices of the boys in the front room. To hear Peter laugh again gave her great satisfaction. Truly he'd been through much for a lad of nine (going on ten). With Alison and Jamie occupied in their rooms, she confronted the problem of the radio interview; wishing Alan would call and take charge. The phone broke her reverie. She reached for it. "Hello, Oh Alan it must be mental telepathy we're having. I was wishing you'd call. How did you get along at work; were the boys hard on you? Did you get much ribbing? Well, that's what I thought. They're a great bunch of fellows you work with. They know you enough to believe in you."

Alan Maitland on the line asked the perfunctory questions about the welfare of his family and what was on Agnes's mind.

"Well," she began, "Peter has some school chums in the front room asking him all sorts of questions. I can hear their excited voices and they're laughing like they're having the time of their lives. It's good for Peter, Alan. He was afraid to face them, but now that its done, he's surprising me with his self assurance. He's holding the floor, that I promise you.

"What I was wishing you'd call is that a Mr. William Bremner phoned from Radio Clyde, Station 102.5, and wants to interview us here in the house. Now, Alan," she interrupted her husband's blustery 'NO WAY.' "He seems like a perfectly good man. He interpreted the telly interview as putting us down as gullible folk wanting attention. . He wants to bring phone lines here and give folk opportunities to call and ask direct questions. He feels this is the only way we'll come across as credible and get better acceptance than what we're getting from the T.V. Interview. We'll be able to answer questions and put some sort of a face to Peter's experience. People aren't daft, Alan, they can tell when they're being conned or not."

When she finished, Alan reflected on her logic. "Aye, hen, I guess you're right as usual. It's just that I hate to be put on the spot by some smarmy man who uses us to get ratings up at our expense. But after talkin' wi' the fellows at work, I know we have to put some kind of an end to this, or we'll be hounded to death by charlatans trying to make gain at our expense.

132

If ye'r comfortable about that chap Bremner, I say go ahead and give him the O.K. to come. Let's get it over wi' as soon as possible. I'm longin' to get back to being ourselves again. Let them what wants it, have all the fame and notoriety they kin get. As for me and my house I'm more than satisfied to be just plain Alan Maitland wi' a fine wife and bonny children. I've learned to appreciate being a nobody to outsiders as long as I'm a somebody to my ain hoose. So we've gained in that department. As Bobby Burns says 'A man's a man for aw' o that.'"

Agnes put the phone on its cradle and went humming around the table picking up the dishes and getting the soapy water ready to wash them. She liked her hands in the soapy water (at times) when she was deep in thought. The suds cleared her mind as if washing crumbs out of her brain. She drained the dishes, slowly dried and put them away. Still humming an unknown melody, she wiped the vinyl tablecloth and went slowly upstairs to her room. Both Jamie's and Alison's doors were shut. She passed them and turned into her and Alan's bedroom shut the door, and proceeded to tidy herself up. She marveled at her actions. She was not planning anything, yet she was acting as if plans were already forming for action.

After dressing, she returned to the kitchen and then to the front room. The boys were sprawled on the floor and Peter was holding 'court.' He was enjoying himself. He was the center of attention. Agnes spoke, "I think it's time you young lads went out to play. The day's a good one for biking. Why not enjoy these last few days before school takes up?"

The boys looked at each other and then at Peter. "He has become their leader" mused his mother. "How long will it last?" Peter acknowledged their stares, shrugged his shoulders and said "Let's go round the Clyde." In no time at all, the front room was empty and the boys plus Peter, were peddling down the road in search of the River Clyde's biking path.

Agnes reminisced. Life was becoming a little more normal. Now for calling Mr. Bremner and making an appointment. She reached for the phone, dialed the radio station's number, and was shortly speaking directly with William Bremner. "We've decided to take you up on your offer, Mr. Bremner," Agnes informed him. "My husband would like to have it done as quickly as possible and get the matter laid to rest."

"I quite agree with Mr. Maitland" was the reply. "We can have our phone lines installed when you give us the go-ahead; the sooner the better. Shall we say this afternoon. We can be ready by the time your husband comes home from work. How does that suit you?"

Agnes was a little flustered at the shortness of time for her to get the family ready. Then she mused. "We're not going on the telly, no one will see what we look like or how the house looks, so the sooner the better. We'll have less time to fret." She told Mr. Bremner that his suggestion would be perfectly acceptable. He seemed delighted. Said he'd be there with his men no later than 2:30 that afternoon. He hung up after thanking her.

Agnes called to Jamie and Alison; "We're being interviewed this afternoon by Mr. William Bremner of Radio Clyde here in Glasgow." She stopped. Neither child was impressed, rather they looked uninterested. The television interview had made them feel daft and they were not anxious to repeat the experience. "Mum," protested Alison, " do we have to go through that again?"

" Yes, it's worrisome I know but we have to get this sighting of Nessie put to rest. It won't be anything like the BBC interview; we'll not be on camera and we will be answering folk that call in about the sighting. I believe it will clear up misunderstandings some folk feel about Peter's sighting and we'll be able to get back to being normal."

"Do you think we'll ever be able to be just normal again?" queried Jamie. "I think so" murmured Agnes.

But she also had her doubts.

Chapter 5

Shortly before 2 o'clock a huge van with the radio station's logo on its side, made its way up Glamis Road stopping in front on #7. Agnes, with a clean frock on, her red hair brushed and neatly in place, parted the lace curtains and watched as three men began unloading cables and wires and telephone equipment. "My, all of that for an interview" she mused. "'Of course they need those for incoming lines." She continued to watch as the truck disgorged heavy cable lines and string them along the side of the house. When the bell rang, she found a short grey headed and grey bearded man on the stoop.

Hat in hand, the man proffered his hand and introduced himself as William Bremner. Agnes blushed slightly at his courteous manner and ushered him into the front room. He declined her offer to sit down with, "I'd love to Mrs. Maitland, but I must make certain that we're hooked up to have four incoming lines. If we only have two, folk will hang up if they get a busy signal. With at least four lines they're not as apt to get a busy signal for long." He took his leave and she watched as he directed his men connect the lines; bringing some into the living room. She went in search of her family.

Peter returned in time to see the finishing of the telephone lines in and around his house. He rushed in shouting, "Mum, where's everybody and what's going on?"

His mother called him upstairs. "We're going on the radio when your dad comes home. The wires are for extra telephone lines so people can call in and ask questions."

"Oh no," Peter exploded. "I don't want to answer anymore questions about Nessie. I wish I'd never seen her. I'm sick to death of all the hubbub. No one believes me. When I was talking wi' my friends at times I dinna ken if they believed me. Can't we just forget about it and go back to being normal?"

"It's not that easy, son. Curiosity is what keeps us all going. People's imaginations are never filled. They need to be fed new things all the time. It's what makes us people and not animals. Right now, Nessie has become alive in many minds. Of course the skeptics will never believe, but it's not those we need to help, it's the folk who have imagination and get a feeling of being right about their favorite fantasy. Nessie is the most talked about mystery in all of Scotland; in fact all of Europe when you come to think of it.

"We can be oorsel's, in our own front room. No telly cameras glaring down at us. All you need to do is be honest about what you saw. You don't add to or take anything away from it. You'll see, by doing this, the curious will hopefully be satisfied and we'll be off the hook. You'll do us proud, Peter, I know you will." Agnes reached for her son and hugged him. "You seem so much more grown up these days," she told him. Peter flushed with pleasure.

True to his word, Alan was home early; having urged one of his mates to finish the last of his bread route. He glanced at the cables and phone extensions and bolted up the stairs looking for Agnes. She was leaving the loo when he got to the top and he ushered her into the bedroom. "Why all the phone wires; its a wire jungle doon there"

"Mr. Bremner said he wanted four open lines for folk to call in and not get the busy signal all the time. He's quite a nice chap, Alan. He's not a bit smarmy; all business. Really nice," she concluded. "Just wash up and come down. No need to get over dressed; we're not on the telly. Praise the Lord for that blessing." She kissed him on the cheek and descended the stairs. Alan looked after her admiring her calm. He shrugged his shoulders and went into the loo.

Entering the front room, she espied Mr. Bremner on his knees sorting out some wires around a circle of chairs. "Ah there you are, Mrs. Maitland' he smiled. "just making sure connections are properly hooked up. I thought we'd be comfortable sitting in this position so we'd not get tangled up with the wires. This box is our speaker." He pointed to a square object resting in the middle of the coffee table. Four telephones were placed for easy access.

"We'll all be able to hear what each caller says and answer from the hand phones. It will go well. I don't anticipate your family being phone shy. I admired their poise on BBC, so I know they'll do fine in this set up." He smiled encouragingly and turned to continue his investigation of the hook ups.

Leaving the front room Agnes went up the stairs in search of her family. She found Jamie and Alison and Peter in their rooms and Alan she heard washing up in the loo. She called the children into her room. "Mr. Bremner is a very pleasant and genuinely nice man. He won't smirk at your answers to any questions the callers ask you. He wants this to be a win for him and a win for us. His station is the first to ask us and so we want to do our best to honor the faith he is showing in bringing his crew here instead of us having to go to the radio station. Now don't be scared. All I'm asking is that you be polite even when some questions make you mad. And some probably will." She looked at her watch then shooed them down the stairs. She knocked at the door of the loo and told Alan they'd see him downstairs.

When the family was seated , Mr. Bremner gave instructions as to how to answer the questions; to watch his hand for clues as to when to speak and when to finish. Asking if there were any questions the children and adults shook their heads and acknowledged their understanding of his instructions. Agnes had already been clued. William Bremner warned them that there might be cranks calling in for no other reason than to be nuisances. "In a talk show format, the weirdoes come out in great numbers. But decent folk also take a spell at calling in to express opinions or ask questions. We'll have some of both. It's our hope and prayer that we have more decent folk than cranks tonight. However just keep your cool, answer their questions and don't get mad. If your voice sounds angry you've had it with your audience. They expect you to take all kinds of flack and still be able to quit ye like men."

Bremner's assurance and explanations excited them and when air time signal was given, they were eager to answer one and all; to take on cranks and commoners in stride.

When ON THE AIR signal flashed, William Bremner began his peroration with "Good afternoon my faithful radio audience. This is William Bremner speaking for Radio Station Clyde, l02.5 on your dial. It's a special privilege I have to be able to tell you that at this moment I am seated in the living room of the Maitland family here in Glasgow. You will remember their nine year old son, Peter, who just a short week ago met Nessie when she took an evening stroll near his uncle's home in Inverness. There are many stories circulating concerning the authenticity of such a sighting . It is Station Clyde's privilege to have them answer your questions direct. Please speak your name and be as brief with the wording of your question, for we have but one hour to cover a multitude of inquiries. You may speak to any of the children; Peter; age nine;

excuse me, he wants you to know he will soon be ten, then Jamie; fifteen, and Alison; thirteen. Thank you for tuning in to Radio Station l02.5." Here Mr. Bremner gave the station's phone numbers.

Background music was soon interrupted by the ringing of phones. "Good afternoon, may I have your name and question please," began Bremner.

" I'm Angus Brown from Glasgow and I'd like to have the wee lad explain how the beastie could walk. I thought she was water bound."

Mr. Bremner nodded to Peter who took up a phone. "I can tell you that I saw the beastie walking on what looked like stumpy flippers."

Mr. Brown persisted. "Has anyone ever seen a picture of Nessie on land?" Here Peter looked appealingly to Jamie for help. Mr. Bremner nodded to Jamie.

"This is Jamie speaking, Mr. Brown. I've done some research on land sightings since Peter saw Nessie, and there is one book that deals with land sightings by a Mrs. Constance Whyte. She records the names of folk who saw the monster on land. I found other such information on the web sight under Loch Ness Monster land sightings. No one expected to see the beastie so didn't have a camera ready."

The next caller wanted to know what length and color the beastie was. Here Peter could answer with great clarity. "Nessie has a leathery body kinda gray, with a long neck and a wee head. It dragged its body on stumpy flippers."

Peter grinned across at his mum saying in essence, "I got through that one alright." Agnes smiled back in understanding."

One caller wanted to know what was the best time to get a glimpse of Nessie in the loch.

Jamie picked this up by reciting information gleaned from Frank Searle's book 'Around Loch Ness.' Mr. Searle is regarded highly by Nessie fans. He has spent thousands of hours out on the water in a small boat. He has made over twenty eight sightings and taken pictures on eight different occasions. He is judged to be a qualified writer regarding Nessie. Mr. Searle says there is no set time. You could sit down on the bank for ten minutes and catch a glimpse of Nessie. On the other hand you could sit for hours and days and not see anything. There's no particular season either that is best for seeing the beastie."

Alan and Agnes nodded to each other and cocked their heads toward Jamie as if to say. "We've got a smart one here." Neither parent was aware of the notes Jamie had gathered on his visit to the library.

It was evident to Mr. Bremner that one of the Maitland children had done his homework. He was impressed and relieved. His concern had been that the callers would make mince meat out of the children with their sarcastic and snide remarks of unbelief. Bremner smiled to himself. He had taken a chance by the faith he'd observed in the Maitlands' credibility when they'd been under scrutiny on BBC Television. His hunch was paying off. The station's ratings would get a much needed boost. However, he knew that ratings were not primary in his choice of asking the family to appear on the air. He'd felt sorry for their treatment by the uppity BBC chairman.

The next questioner introduced himself as James Russell. "What 's the sense in draggin' up this auld story aboot a beastie in the loch. We've been weaned on it. It's no news anymore. My question to any one is; "What are ye gettin' to appear on the telly and noo the radio. Who's gettin' rich oot of these wains bein' put up to such nonsense?"

Alan Maitland's face got so red Agnes feared an explosion. Mr. Bremner held up his hand in caution. "Mr. Maitland would you like to address this caller?"

"Och, aye," said Alan; his idiomatic Scottish brogue hanging out like a red flag. "I'll be glad to let this gent know just how we've benefited by all this marvelous publicity. Well sir, we've been surrounded in oor hoose by sight seekers and hecklers every time we go out or come in. Oor phone is never silent; it insults us when we pick it up. Once in a while we have a remark of confidence, but these have been few and far between. We're called adventurers, limelight seekers and deceivers. Have we filled oor pockets wi' loot? Not unless ye count the fact that we canna go oot shoppin' so we're not spendin' oor pay as easily. That could be called money in the pocket; but it's oor ain money we're not spendin' Oor family stays indoors;

no wantin' to be followed and made fun of. I do have something' to be thankful for. The lads I've worked wi' for years support me and havny let me doon. If I was heckled at work, I dinny know how I'd be able to support my family. Yes, sir, we've benefited but it's all been negative. If ye'd like to change places wi' us, bc oor guest. Ye could say a wee prayer for us, as we try to get back to normal from an experience my wee son had; not of his choosing."

Mr. Bremner was visibly moved by Alan's remarks. He cleared his throat; an action that caused the three children to think of Uncle Sam when he was emotionally touched.

One caller took up their cause."Hello, my name's Elspeth Burns and I live in Paisley. I've been a follower of Nessie sightings for years. Some of my friends have actually seen Nessie in the loch.. I've also read Whyte's book on land sightings that young Jamie referred to. I've promoted interest in Nessie but have come to the conclusion that not many have faith in unusual phenomena. It's been a real thrill to hear about Peter's experience. It's given me renewed interest. I can only say, 'God bless you all' and somehow something will turn up to validate Peter's sighting."

How true was Mrs. Burns' prognostication. Validation would make it's appearance, but not before anguish and rejection made theirs first.

'My name's Archie McKay, from Glasgow. My question is how did these strange creatures get into the loch in the first place?" Jamie was once more given the nod.

"The theory goes that these creatures once went in and out of the loch from the North Sea for feeding on the loch's fish. There was some local land upheaval in the area and the creatures in the loch at that time got trapped. They couldn't get back to the North Sea."

"But," argued McKay, "how could they exist so long. I've heard aboot them since I was four; now I'm 84. Me faither heard aboot them from his faither. So how could these beasties still be alive after hundreds and even thousands of years?"

"Mr. McKay," said Jamie; "I looked for that answer too. Some marine biologists wrote that a minimum of fourteen such creatures could keep the species going. Of course they don't know how many are in the loch, no one has been able to study the creatures. But we have to acknowledge by the thousands of sightings over the years that these creatures are still alive in the loch."

"Thank ye laddie, I appreciate your candor. I'll be reading up on old Nessie. I used to follow the sightings, then got upset wi' some of the hoaxes that were played on the public by some pranksters." Mr. McKay broke his connection with "God bless ye."

"Ruby Young from Kirkcaldy and I'm enjoying hearing about oor Nessie. Is it true that more than one beastie has been seen at a time? I'd like to hear from Jamie."

"Yes, two and even three have been seen together. Folk in the know think they travel in families." Mrs. Young persisted; 'What reason do writers give for them coming up to the surface?"

Again Jamie answered. "There are plenty of chard, eel , etc. fish in the loch. Salmon swim closer to the surface than most other of the fish the monsters like to eat. The belief is that they surface for salmon."

"Thank you young man. Your parents should be very proud of you." To this compliment, Jamie blushed a bright red.

Agnes and Alan looked a bit concerned. Jamie was in the limelight because of his knowledge. Peter, the one who was the reason of all this attention was being almost ignored . Their faces registered their concern. William Bremner took note and took charge.

"Peter, tell us how it felt to be in the presence of such a large creature. How has it affected your life."

Peter flushed with pleasure as he turned and addressed the box. "I was as scared as I could be when I was sitting on my bum looking up at this huge creature. At first I was so flummoxed that I didna believe my eyes. The thought crossed my mind that it might drop the wee sheep and swing its long neck around and grab me instead. Now that it's in the past I can understand folk not believing my tale. I sometimes have to pinch myself to make me relive it. It seems so impossible to have happened. But it did happen. I ran screaming to Uncle Sam's. He and the others came with torches

147

and we roped off the place where the beastie walked. Whenever I think I dreamed the whole thing I remember that awful trampled mess of trees and bushes. Then, I canna' forget the wee sheep's bleating'. The little bell around its neck sounded so sad and seemed to be asking for help. It's not been easy to keep all these things in my mind with so many folk telling me I'm making it up for publicity. If that was the case it wouldn't be worth it." Here Peter shook his head and looked solemnly at his folk and Mr. Bremner.

The red signal flashed insistently. Mr. Bremner nodded to it and to himself. It had been so successful. More than he'd dreamed of.

"We bring our interview of the Maitland family to a close, but before we go, I would ask Alison if she had a word to contribute."

Alison, so pleased, looked at her mum and dad and then Mr. Bremner. "It has not been easy for any of us to hear the hecklers make fun of Peter. We saw the destruction in Nessie's wake. We believed in his sighting. He's no perfect, but he's no liar. I just wished folk would give us a bit of breathing room after our experience. Peter seeing the monster has affected us all. We go to school next week and we're not sure of how we'll be received. We don't want to be celebrities. We just want to be accepted as we were before Nessie entered our lives."

Mr. Bremner ended the broadcast with "A good day to all from Radio Clyde; 105.2 on your dial. Listen in tomorrow, same time, same station for up to date news and events."

The silence followed was so complete that even breathing paused in the air not wanting to break the moment.

" Whew". Peter broke the silence and breathing took its rightful place. The people in the room looked at each other as if for the first time recognizing that a monumental happening had taken place; and they were at the center.

Alison giggled, then looked sheepishly at her mum and dad. Agnes stood up and stated "It's time for tea and we'd be honored if you'd join us, Mr. Bremner."

William Bremner's sigh was one of contentment. "I'd be pleased to accept your invitation. Let me first get my lads to undo their handiwork and get these contraptions out of your living room." He bustled around finding his men and giving orders.

Alan, finding himself out on a limb, followed his wife into the kitchen asking if he could help. "Yes see that Jamie and Peter are all right. Alison will give me help in the kitchen. Alison, get the good bone china cups out of the china cabinet. Take a clean towel and dust them out. They've not been used since Auntie Barbara was here last January. There's a lass."

Agnes bustled around filling the kettle, looking into the frig to see what delicacy she could concoct out of a nearly bare refrigerator. Going to the store had proven to be such a hazard that she'd almost run out of staples. She took a tin of salmon, opened it, drained it and separated the bones from the pink fish. To it she added a drop of lemon and made salmon sandwiches. Finding a bit of lettuce she added to the sandwiches. Her Sultana cake baked for last Christmas' holidays was still fresh as she always wrapped it in muslin and kept it in a tin with a tight cover. She added some scones and marmalade to the set table. She put out her best silverware and made tea when the kettle shrieked that its water was boiling. Filling her largest teapot, she put a cosey on it; set it on the trivet on the sideboard. She went to assemble her men folk and Mr. Bremner.

Mr. Bremner asked for permission to wash up. He was shown where the loo was. They were soon seated around the sparse but adequate table with a grateful Alan saying a small grace.

Mr. Bremner said "Amen."

" I can truthfully tell you folk that I was extremely concerned about how this interview would go. I've had many that turned out so badly that at times I declared I'd have no more interviews. You folk have restored my faith in the ability of good people to be able to answer questions without being condescending to the caller or try to show off, which comes across clear to listening audiences. I feel that the guid Lord was doing the selecting of callers, for we had barely more than a couple who took umbrage at the sighting of Nessie. I tell you, my heart was in my throat every time a phone rang. I must commend Peter for enduring the criticisms, and they're not over with yet. You came across as an ordinary lad who believed what he was saying. That made the listeners believe. They did not hear any uncertainty in your voice; you spoke the truth as you knew it. It came across.

"I must also commend Jamie for being alert and looking up facts at the library. They were invaluable. People like points of reference; not just hearsay or opinions. The library will probably get many calls for Whyte's book and the Internet will be used to look up additional resources. Alison's closing remarks were excellent; they spoke of the problems you have faced and of the concern for school days ahead. These are points of anxiety that most people can identify, and sympathize with. I believe you did your brothers and yourself much good by your sincere remarks.

"And Alan, I congratulate you for heeding my hand and not succumbing to anger when that blethering idiot asked about using your family for gain. You stated your position and gave us all something to think about. Surely you have all been under a strain and have suffered undeservedly. This message will do you all much good.

"Mrs. Maitland, yours was the hardest task of all; keeping silent. You agonized for each member as he took a question and I'm sure were praying mightily while your husband with his face as red as a beet talked to the caller. You know, the Bible verse that came to me while I watched you (my mither brought us up wi' verses from the Bible) this he spoke in the Scottish vernacular…was 'They also serve who stand and wait'. You stood and waited. Thank you so much for this grand tea, but I must hurry on out and let my lads get to their homes and their teas. I canna' be greedy, now can I?" He grinned impishly and went out.

When Mr. Bremner left their home, it was as if an old friend had departed. They'd known him such a short time, but had found in him an honorable and somehow the word 'righteous man', seemed to fit him.

There was much to talk about when left by themselves, but no one was talking. Each was reliving (inwardly) his/her reply to callers. This experience would last them a long time. Agnes broke into their reverie with, "It's been a hard week for us all, but we've grown stronger for the experience. We're set apart right now, and will always be that 'Maitland family whose wee son said he saw oor Nessie'. We don't understand why Peter was chosen to see Nessie, but he was. So now, we'll never be one of the ordinary folk. We've had an outstanding experience that's put us above the fray. When things get hard for you, remember the guid Lord had His hand in all of this, and take comfort in it. I don't know about you, but I'm fixing to go to bed early tonight after the news."

Alan reached over and caught Agnes's hand in his. "Hen what would we do without yer sane approach to life. I've been sittin' brooding' and trying to control my restlessness, and oot comes the very words that bring understanding to this muddle we've been in. O' course we're different; and I guess we canna have it both ways. We canna be like all the others and still live wi' Nessie in oor hoose. So I reckon I'll just choose to be laughed at and lied aboot. I'll just take the taunts and wear 'em as badges. Peter, Jamie and Alison, I suggest ye listen good to yer smart wee mum. Especially when yer facing yer friends and enemies at school."

It was sound advice. However, as the saying goes, 'It's easier telt than felt'.

Before the news came on the phone rang. Agnes, nearest to it answered with a 'Hello, this is Agnes Maitland."

"Mrs. Maitland" a deep voice stated, "This is John McKenzie Head Master at Knox Secondary School. I'm wanting to see Alison and Jamie in my office Tuesday. As you know school commences Monday but for the teaching staff only. The students report on Tuesday morning at the regular time of 8;15. I'm really seeking your permission to talk with your children before their school mates pester them with questions. What I have in mind is scheduling a question and answer period in the school auditorium for Tuesday afternoon. This will be announced at the start of school and the students will be forestalled from asking any questions ahead of time. I'm quite anxious that the school beginning should not be interrupted by the furor over the sighting. I will be advising the teaching staff of my intention and they can be on their guard against any breakage of this order of school policy. I have been in contact with Headmaster A. Andrew McCrindle of Peter's primary school. I have his cooperation to allow Peter and his class to participate, Peter, of course, being the main attraction.

"I want to commend you folk for your excellent participation on Station Clyde this afternoon. You certainly did credit as a good model family for us here in Glasgow. We need families like yours to hold up the sagging image the television displays of family life here in Glasgow. Do I have your permission to hold this interview with your children?"

Agnes paused but only for one second. "I think it's a splendid idea. I've been concerned about the interruption of the school day myself. This relieves my mind. Thank you for asking permission. Should I prepare my children or would you rather tell them when they come to your office?"

"Just tell them to come and see me when the bell rings. I suggest they get here just as the bell rings, if that is possible. I'll be on the lookout for them or one of the teachers, if I'm elsewhere. Good talking with you, Mrs. Maitland. Good evening."

Agnes was deep in thought when Alan persisted; "Who was on the phone? I've asked you twice." "Sorry, I didn't hear you Alan. That was the Head Master at Jamie's and Alison's school and he wanted to know."......She related the conversation and the plan Mr. McKenzie had delineated. Alan was both pleased and proud. Then he worried; would the lassies and lads poke fun at his children? He remembered the dour Head Master, and felt better. He'd be a match for any heckler or sneerers'. Alan whistled 'Bluebells of Scotland.' Agnes smiled. He's feeling happy and proud; the song was his harmony of comfort and peace.

After an early bedtime, the family was up early. It was Saturday and bed did not claim their bodies as it did work or school days. Agnes had shoes to buy for the boys; and a new jumper for Alison. Ordinarily all would have been bought and closeted. But since the children's return from Inverness, Nessie had gotten in the way of shopping. There were no more days, unless she left the shopping 'til Monday, and she frowned at that idea. After a short breakfast, Agnes , already having persuaded Alan to drive them to town, got her family once again in the car. No visitors were at their door. Things just might be returning to normal. Driving to town was a strain on Alan for he despised Saturday traffic; especially town traffic. His mood was dour, but bearable.

"I'll let you off at Suchihaul Street and you can wander the shops by yourselves . I'm taking the car and parking it and I'll try to find a no' too busy barber. I look like a mod bloke. I'll pick you up aboot when?"

Agnes thought. "Give me two hours. If we find what we need quicker than that, we'll go into a tea shop. Where will you be picking us up?"

Alan stopped in front of a hotel. He pointed. "I'll circle the block here, if yer no' here in two hours." He kissed Agnes and waved at his family as they departed the car. On he went to look for a "No too busy barber on a Saturday morning."

Shopping was always tiring especially when trying to find shoes a pocketbook could afford. They were so dear these days. Agnes allowed more for the purchases than she would normally have done. First, she was tired from the week's activities, and second, she'd been able to put away more because of their inability to get out of the house. Alison's jumper took more time. She was growing up and was more choosey than usual. The boys got impatient with her. After several stores, she found a jumper she could be satisfied with. They left the stores with their parcels. Agnes looked for a tea shop. They still had forty five minutes before going to the front of the designated hotel.

The respite from shopping was comforting and enjoyable. They had chosen their drinks and a scone and were just biting into it when a voice interrupted eating progress. "Agnes, where have ye been hidin' yersel? Havny seen ye since ye were on the telly." The owner of the voice was Mrs. Brown one of their neighbors.

Agnes smiled and went on drinking her tea; attempting to put off any interrogation her nosy neighbor might be attempting. "Oh, we've been awful busy with getting the children's school clothes and all. How is your family, Helen. I haven't seen them around either. Did you get to Saltcoats on your holiday? You mentioned you were planning on going?" Agnes did her best to shift the object of conversation from her own family to that of her neighbor's. Mrs. Brown wasn't falling for that ploy. "Oh, we went on holidays alright but nothing exciting happened to us as it did to yer own wee family. How are ye Peter? Are ye over yer fright at seeing the beastie?'"

Peter gulped down his scone with a drink of milk and answered. "Yes, Mrs. Brown I'm over the fright, but will never forget it."

Before Mrs. Brown could launch into another question Jamie pointed out the window. "Mum, I just saw Dad pass the window in the car I think he's looking for us. We'd best be going, eh?"

Agnes drank the last of her tea and put the rest of her scone in the paper napkin. Putting down a tip for the waitress she stood up and shooed her brood out of the tea shop leaving a frowning Mrs. Brown looking after them.

Once outside, they made their way down to where Alan had said he'd meet them. It was less than five minutes before he circled around. They got into the car and were off home. "Whew" cried Alison, "we just left nosey Mrs. Brown in the tea shop. If Jamie hadn't spotted you, she'd still be grilling us."

Alan looked back at Jamie. Jamie ducked his head. "This is the first time I've been around the block. I didny pass any tea shop. But then maybe a car just like mine did and that's what Jamie saw."

On the way home Agnes felt the pit of her stomach churn within; Nessie was invading more than their public privacy. She was invading the area Agnes cared more about than anything. Integrity and honesty. True, Jamie had helped them escape an unpleasant situation with Mrs. Brown, but at a price Agnes was not willing to pay for her brood. She wrestled silently with such thoughts. Was she being overly alarmed? After all, today people lied without thinking of consequence nor apologized when caught in a lie. The school was always having to suspend students for cheating and lying to cover up. She would talk with Alan and get him to have a father to son discussion.

Reaching 7 Glamis, they were grateful to find an absence of cars and sightseers at their door. "Maybe we'll be left alone" this from Alison. She sounded a bit wistful, for the notoriety had been one of delight to an impressionable budding teenager. She basked in the overflow of attention that mainly centered around Peter and of late, Jamie. She would not have admitted it, but she was feeling immensely important and wanted this aura to translate to popularity when she returned to school.

"I have a notion that folk have something noo to gawk at by this time" stated her father. This notion put Alison's popularity dream in the midden before it had fully developed.

He continued, "I can only thank the guid Lord for peace at last. It's ver' good to take my family into the hoose withoot havin' some bugger put a camera or a mike in my face and expected to answer questions I'd never thought of before. Och aye I'm done wi' being interviewed."

Salmon sandwiches, tea and milk was their late afternoon meal. Saturday night was their busiest; clothes to iron, shoes to polish; hair to wash and braid and baths to be taken. Sunday revolved around going to the kirk.

The initial shock of the Maitland's 'seeing Nessie' over, the congregation treated them without fuss and fanfare. This was comforting and made worship all the easier. They appreciated the friendship of the church's congregation. Questions had been asked about the sighting, but with tact. Going to the kirk now posed no problem.

With the children upstairs tending to their Saturday chores, Agnes broached the subject of Jamie's 'wee story' to Alan. His reaction was typical. His face turned red with annoyance at being faced with an unpleasant task. At first he scoffed at the significance of the 'wee story'. "Hen" he comforted, "we're no raisin' angels in this hoose. Sure he told a wee fib, but didny you all benefit by it? Come on, hen, Jamie's a truthful lad; this'll no' damage that. Let's just leave well enough alone, eh?"

Agnes got up from the table, picked up the dirty dishes and moved toward the sink. With the table cleared she filled the sink with warm soapy water. She did most of her thinking with her hands in dishwater.

"Och aye," she remarked savagely to the innocent dishes in the soapy water. "No big deal; really. He did us all a grand favor gettin' us oot of a sticky situation. O' course when another one comes along, he'll no be thinkin' of repeating his actions, 'cause he kens we never approved his lying today. Things will right themselves. The next time the family has a problem we'll just call on Jamie to get us oot of a worrisome situation."

Alan got up and came over to the sink. He stood behind her and brought her hands out of the water and turned her around. 'I'm sorry lass, I wasn'y thinking past my nose. I ken where yer' goin' wi' this. Yer right. I'll get myself upstairs and have a wee chat wi' oor smart, honest young lad. But for goodness sakes lass, dinny scare me like ye did the noo. When ye begin to talk in yer native tongue, man o' man that puts the wind up me." He kissed her cheek and left the room.

"Alan," she called after him. "don't be too hard on him, he meant well."

Alan's laugh could be heard as he bounded up the stairs. "Women," he shouted back down, "who can understand them." Agnes smiled enigmatically.

"How come it takes this family so long to get ready for the kirk?" snapped Alan as his family was finally seated in the car. Agnes gave him her penetrating look that warned him to go no further with his tirade. The last minute "Mum have you seen my new tie? Mum where's my clean shirt? Mum my shoe lace just broke. Mum, my new shoes are too tight. Mum, my cow lick won't stay down. Mum can you braid- my hair'...etc." Same characters; same voices, but different needs were the fare of Sunday's getting her family ready for the kirk.

Agnes remembered her own childhood experiences. Remembered her own mum's admonitions when the siblings fought in the back seat of the car on the way to the kirk. "Ye can kill yersel's on the way" her mother would calmly state, "but yer all goin' to the kirk. The Devil isny' going to get the upper hand wi' this family."

She laughed silently at her mother's terse remarks. She understood now what her parents had gone through just to get them to the kirk on Sunday. She now appreciated their strength of endeavor. They wanted their family to factor God into their lives. Reminiscing her childhood did not however make her feel more kindly toward Alan. Her warning look had shut him up. He began to hum 'Bluebells of Scotland' as he smiled her way.

After a bit of driving, Agnes glanced back at her 'creations'. They looked clean, pressed, and beautiful.

"I wouldny change place wi' the Queen of England," she breathed to herself in thanksgiving to the Giver of life. Her surreptitious glance at Jamie brought his gaze to her. He smiled sheepishly. Alan's talk with him had settled the matter. Jamie understood. He was also thankful for parents who cared enough to steer him from taking the wrong turn in the future.

Reaching the kirk, Alan let his family out at the front door. He proudly watched as they walked toward the kirk. He waved to some friendly folk, then sought a place to park.

With Sunday School over, Agnes and Alan sat in the auditorium waiting to be joined by their children. Agnes was deep in contemplation as the organist played her favorite hymn; 'How firm a foundation.' The words were so beautiful. She repeated them silently to match the beautiful strain. The foundation, that's it she remarked silently. "This is what we're striving for in the lives of our children; a foundation to stand on." Often she'd been bombarded by friends who had fallen for the philosophy of not making children go to Sunday School or the kirk against their will. "Children must be given the freedom of choice" was the mantra many of their friends had fallen for. Agnes, not one to withhold her opinion when it was challenged. She countered back with. "And I suppose you let your children make up their minds about attending their school?" was her favorite retort. "You send them to school whether they like it or not. If you have to drag them oot o' their bed in the morning and shove them oot the door they go. Sick or no sick. Och aye; they go. Where's the consistency in your logic? School feeds their minds (or so it's supposed to). Well, in my book and in my mither's; Sunday School and kirk feeds their everlasting souls." Agnes's remarks usually put closure to the conversation.

The children soon filed into the pew and again both parents glanced with pride at their 'creations.' They knew full well that many eyes were on their backs. Curiosity was still ripe; but it was friendlier curiosity than their first return after the advent of 'Nessie.'

The minister was a white headed man who believed in the 'Good Book' and kept his congregation informed as to its contents. He was not a great orator. He was just a simple servant plying his faith for the building up of his 'sheep' as he so often called his congregation. There were some who wanted someone 'more in touch with the times.' "Whatever that means" was Alan's terse remark when he heard such statements. "Heaven is still up there" he would say and "we're all wantin' to get there. Hell's still in the same place, and we ken we dinna want to go there. So what's the big deal aboot the minister changing and becoming more 'modern'. I dinna ken. If the gospel has changed so that we need a new approach that's something. But for my small knowledge of the Scriptures, the Bible still has the same do's and don'ts as it's always had. I'm, no wantin' any new fangled philosophies for my family. I'll stick wi' a minister who can withstand all the new fangled babble and claptrap, in spite of bricks thrown his way." Alan was not given over to spiritualizing events; but he could hold his own when his way of thinking was challenged. He was the silent bulwark of the family; Agnes was the more vocally fluid.

The sermon had reached its conclusion; the congregation stood for dismissal. Prayer was given; the Doxology sung and the people left their pews slowly. The church emptied with the organ softly playing 'What a Friend We Have in Jesus'.

The family was stopped time after time by friends who had heard the radio broadcast .

"Heard the radio broadcast; it was wonderful. You should be proud of Jamie's answers; and of course Peter, who started this all. And Alison I thought your last remark was just lovely."

The kindness of their fellow worshipers remained with them as they drove out of the kirk. "Ye ken, hen," remarked Alan "Sometime I canny stand a lot of those folk, but when pushes come to shoves, it's those ye find in the kirk what will stand wi' ye."

Agnes had no rebuttal. She was glad they'd gotten to the kirk; heard a good sermon; and sung praises to God. Her family was strengthened. That was what was important.

"What do ye say if we drop by Scotty's and pick up fish and chips for our dinner?"

"Great, I'm starved," stated Alison.

Alan looked back at Alison and remarked "Ye look plenty well fed to me. But we'll make a hurried trip so you won't expire in oor back seat." Getting the nod from his wife, he made a quick turn to the left and drove to the best fish and chip place in the town.

Agnes usually had Sunday dinner in the oven and would not have countenanced such a suggestion; but the week's upheaval had taken the starch out of her and she'd laid in very little food for her flock.

The interior of the car smelled deliciously of the fish and chips that were held in brown paper bags by their mother's steady hands. Around the hastily set table (unmatched dishes and cutlery) a short grace was said by Alan and the family soon made short shrift of the aromatic fish and chip dinners piled on their plates.

"If we hadn'y been so hungry" remarked Alan, "I would have recited Bobby Burn's favorite grace." The family groaned; they knew it by hear. Without prompting they recited in unison:

"Some hae meat and canna eat,

And some wad eat that want it;

But we hae meat and we can eat

So let the Lord be thankit."

The children clapped their hands in glee. It was a good release for the tensions they'd faced that week; and a good under- pinning for the troubles that waited them.

Katie S. Watson

Chapter 6

Monday morning Agnes sat holding her tea cup with both hands, elbows resting on the kitchen table. She'd had a restless night, falling to sleep an hour before the alarm sounded. After getting Alan off to work, she pondered the things she'd need to do before school started Tuesday morning. Alan had promised he'd leave her the car and "bum a ride from one of the blokes," so she could drive the children to their schools in the morning. The two schools were some four miles apart; not much of a juggle, but still time had to be reckoned with if they didn't show up late and not too early either.

Usually Peter took the bus at the corner and Jamie and Alison preferred walking. This scenario would be altered for the first school day. Her musings were interrupted by the ringing of the phone. She quickly reached for it to silence it so that the children could sleep a little longer.

"Mrs. Maitland?" inquired a well-modulated, educated voice. "Yes," she replied. "This is Andrew McCrindle, Headmaster of your son Peter's school." Agnes acknowledged him with a murmur and he continued. "I wonder if we could coordinate the tine of Peter's arrival at school in the morning. We want to spare him any undue pestering by his classmates. I don't want him bullied by some of the rougher boys."

A grip of fear crept over Agnes but she calmed herself and answered serenely. "I plan to drop Peter off at his school and then Jamie and Alison at theirs. What time would you like me to drop him off?"

"I will be on the lookout for him," went on Mr. McCrindle, "and if something happens I'm tied up elsewhere, one of the staff will bring him into my office when he arrives. We will make certain he is taken care of."

Agnes thanked him and said "Good-by." His call had encouraged her but at the same time had sent unpleasant signals through her mind. Was he being an alarmist? she wondered. Why all the caution. She busied herself with the list of things she wanted to do before the phone had rung. She had a difficult time. On her list she jotted down pencils, composition books, erasers for all three children. There her mind went blank; couldn't think of anything else they might need. She put the pad and pencil to one side. As if on cue the phone rang. "I do apologize for bothering you Mrs. Maitland,' said the smooth voice of John McCormick. "I just got off the phone with Mr. McCrindle and he tells me or the arrangements he made with you concerning the arrival of Peter at school in the morning. Do you have any idea what time we can expect to see Jamie and Alison? I don't want them harassed. That might be a hard word, but I want to be on the side of caution."

Agnes once more steadying her nerves spoke into the mouthpiece. "I will drop Peter off at the first bell and bring Jamie and Alison over after that. I do hope they won't be marked tardy if they come in after the bell rings."

"Goodness no, they will not be marked tardy whatever time they arrive. I will inform their homeroom teachers of that fact. No worry there," he said dismissively at such an untenable idea. "Thank you so much for your considerate efforts on our behalf," he said before signing off.

Two Headmasters; both anxious. Have a good day was oxymoronic to say the least.

Before she heard the children stir upstairs, Alan called. He too was full of concerns. "The lads here anticipate trouble for our wains in the morrow. Have ye fixed it up with the schools about the time they should get there?"

Agnes assured him that she had and that he shouldn't worry. The Headmasters had assured her that everything would be under control. No need for her to alarm Alan. He had to keep his mind on his job and not have an accident or they'd all worry.

Monday went by fast. Shopping accomplished; school clothes and shoes checked; lunch eaten and then

Alan home from work. He suggested a drive around the River Clyde and its parks. This would take the edge off of staying home and answering the constant ring of the phone. Each was in agreement and if they thought about the events of the next day school opening, they failed to mention it.

Tuesday morning came. Alan left the car keys on the kitchen table and bolted out the back door to catch his ride. She put the keys in her robe pocket, ate a piece of toast and drank the last of her tea. She said a silent prayer on behalf of her 'creations' that a hedge be put around them. After making their lunches and putting their names on the brown bags, she went silently up the stairs

She knocked first at Alison's door calling "Time to get up luv, get into the loo before the boys are up." She proceeded to the boys' rooms and knocked at each door first calling to Peter then to Jamie. "Peter, Jamie, it's time to rise and shine. Now don't turn over, get your feet on the floor and come down for breakfast."

Down the stairs she went and began fixing breakfast. She returned to listen for activity upstairs. She heard the loo flush and figured at least Alison was up. Not hearing noises from the boys' rooms she climbed the stairs and knocked harder on Peter's door. 'Get up or I'll be in and yank the covers off you.

"Jamie lad, are you up? My legs won't take many more trips up these stairs at my age."

"I'm up, Mum. I'll be down after Alison gets out of the loo." This from Jamie.

Agnes knocked at Peter's door once more and after hearing from him, went down stairs. In half an hour the children were sitting at the table eating their breakfast. Saying nothing. Enveloped in thought.

Carrying their school and lunch bags, they went out to the car and filed in. Agnes had timed their departure to reach Peter's school just as the first bell sounded. Leaving the others in the car, she walked with him toward the front door of the school; heading in the direction of the office. One staff member intercepted her and took Peter in charge. Fighting off an urge to hug him, she patted his shoulder and turned around and went to the car and Jamie and Alison The bell had already rung when she reached their school but there were some stragglers coming up the walk. Agnes did not get out of the car but was relieved to see Headmaster John McCormick approach and lead Alison and Jamie into the school. He turned and smiled broadly and waved a good by.

Agnes returned home feeling she'd been on an all day marathon and had lost. She felt deflated, let down, and sad. Not for herself, but for what she thought her children might be going through.

In the meantime Peter sat, as unobtrusive as possible, in a corner of the office. The secretary informed him that his homeroom teacher was Miss Elspeth Burns and she'd been informed that he was sitting in the office. He would be marked present. Later on he and his class were being bussed to the secondary school for the assembly. "My," the secretary enthused, "aren't you the lucky one to have gotten a glimpse of Nessie?" She beamed at him. Peter squirmed; he felt anything but lucky. He'd change places right now with any of the lads who'd been spared a glimpse of Nessie.

Alison and Jamie were in much the same position in Mr. McCormick's office. They were told that Alison's teacher was a Miss Jean Campbell; Jamie's teacher, a Mr. Ian MacIntosh. They were enrolled and marked present by their respective teachers. Not to worry. was the inference. The assembly, they were told was scheduled when school enrollment was completed; no small task for the first day of a school year.

The Headmaster came through the office at 10:30 after settling registration problems with some teachers and asked his secretary to get him a line. Jamie and Alison heard as he talked with Mr. McCrindle. "We're all set here Andrew. When can we expect the lad and his class to come?" Receiving an answer he closed with "Yes, I agree, but let's not borrow trouble. We will be in the auditorium. Bring your class in and see that Peter is brought to the platform to sit with his brother and sister. Thanks Andrew."

By 11 o'clock Jamie and Alison were seated on the platform watching as the classes filed in; led by their respective teacher. Peter's class arrived with Mr. Andrew McCrindle leading them front and foremost to their reserved section. A no nonsense look on his ruddy face he led Peter to the platform.

John McCorrmick waited until all were seated then stepped to the front of the platform. His perorations began with: "We are fortunate to have on this platform three Glasgow children who were involved this summer in the latest Nessie sighting.   Each will describe what he or she observed. We will begin with introducing Peter, who actually had an encounter with the famous beastie.

"Before Peter begins let me give out a wee bit of advice. Don't any be thinking of having his 15 minutes of fame by using derogatory or rude remarks. If so, I'll be ge'in ye a three day holiday."

Lapsing into idiomatic Scots he caused the auditorium to erupt in laughter and clapping. John Mr.Cormick was considered to be one of the best examples of an impeccable English speaker among his peers.   This departure from his lofty image of stiffness and propriety had a profound impact on the students and they loved it.   Thus, jocularity set the mood stage for the children's testimonies.

Motioning to Peter, he put a mike on his shirt. Facing the filled auditorium he intoned; "Give Peter Maitland a good round of applause for he's been through more than any of you can imagine."

Peter flushed with anxiety, was grateful to the Headmaster for his introduction. He began high pitched and haltingly to tell the story that by now was so repetitive it almost seemed scripted by someone else. Soon he found his normal voice and began.

"At times I wished I'd never seen the beastie. But I did. I didn't want to go to Inverness either but I had to. I found my Auntie Mary and Uncle Sam loving and kind. I went out myself that Friday before dark 'cause I was having problems with my feelings and wanted to be alone. I'd not gone too far from Dream Cottage when I felt the ground shake. I figured it was just a lorry passing on the nearby highway. Then when the trees began to rustle and the bushes began to fall away, I thought maybe hunters were coming through looking for deer. I didny feel frightened I just stopped walking. Then oot of the trees I see a wee head on a long, long neck. I couldny figure oot what it was and although I dinna think I was scared, I stayed where I was. More trees began to sway and bushes shoved aside when oot from them came this awfully big creature. Its neck was long and slim but its body was huge and ugly. It was dragging itsel' along on stumpy legs. Something like short elephant legs. I was so startled that I took a tumble backwards and fell on my bum." (There were titters of laughter and ohs, and ahs, as Peter proceeded).

"I sat looking at the beastie and said to mysel' 'I'm seein' Nessie.' The beastie turned its neck around and gave me a long look." More ohs, and frightened ahs. "I was scared by then cause I didny want it to come after me. I saw a wee lamb hangin' from the beastie's mouth. The wee sheep was bleatin' somethin' awful. The beastie shook it and I heard the wee bell tinkle that was on the lamb's neck. It stopped bleatin'. Having no desire to investigate me further, the monster waddled down to the edge of the loch, stopped for a minute then slid down the bank.

"I ran as fast as I could, but when I got to the embankment, all I could see was a big white wake where something large had plunged into the water. I ram screaming to my family's hoose and told them what I'd seen. I could tell by the look on their faces that they didny believe me."

The Headmaster stopped Peter at that juncture and motioned to Jamie. "I want your reaction and those of your family's when you heard Peter's tale."

We thought Peter was pulling our legs but Uncle Sam is a wise old gent and he calmed Peter down. He sat him down at the kitchen table and had him draw a picture of what he'd seen. Alison and I weren't impressed because it looked like pictures of Nessie we'd seen at the Loch Ness Investigation Bureau. We figured he was drawing from memory the picture on the brochure we'd brought back.. Peter was awful upset at the looks on our faces. Uncle Sam asked him if that was all he could remember. He looked long at his drawing then said 'No, I forgot the wee sheep.' He drew a wee lamb dangling out of the beastie's mouth. When Uncle Sam saw that Peter was dead serious he got some torches and we all went out to the place of the sighting. Sure enough there was a huge path strewn with trees and branches and bushes all matted down. It looked like some kind of a tornado had swept through leaving saplings bent in two. There was no doubt that something had happened to make such a mess of the ground. Uncle Sam sent me back to get a piece of Auntie Mary's clothes line. I ran back and he roped the place off."

Thanking Jamie, Mr. McCormick called on Alison for her input. She adjusted the mike and spoke into it. Her voice wavered and cracked a bit before she got herself in hand.

"Of course, we didn't believe Peter. But on the other hand, we'd never had reason to call him a wee fibber. He looked so hurt when he thought we didn't believe him. He sort of hung his head and muttered 'Ye dinna believe me.' I guess that's when I began to really think he was telling the truth. We went out to the place as Jamie said. Sure enough it looked awfully matted and almost like a hurricane had passed by. Uncle Sam looked for lorry tracks. Of course there were none. He looked for the tracks of hunters but again, couldn't see any. After the rope was in place around the area we went back to the house. Uncle Sam looked up the newspaper's number at Inverness and called them. He didn't tell them why they should come, only that they'd be sorry if they didn't show up. When the news reporter finally came, he was a bit angry as to the reason he'd been called. He didn't believe Peter but went out with us to see the roped off place. After that he changed his attitude and called a photographer. Told him to get out on the double to Dream Cottage. Quite soon a man came with a camera and took a lot of photos. I think it was the same with both men; the turmoil of broken tress trampled bushes that made them believe something big had been there that night."

Alison was interrupted by Mr. McCormick who thanked her and waited until she was seated. He addressed the assembly. "We have just a half of an hour for questions. Raise your hands; speak up and then be seated."

Hands shot up. Questions flowed like water.

"Peter, what was the color of the beastie?"

"Where in Inverness is the best place to see Nessie?"

On and on the questions poured out of the students' mouths. There was genuine interest in their voices; true interest in hearing their answers. It was as if this generation was getting a first hand understanding of the Nessie phenomenon; excited and proud that this beastie belonged to Scotland. Their ain land.

The mood changed dramatically when a cocky voice announced. "My faither thinks it's all a hoax just to get mare visitors up to Inverness. He says yer probably bein' paid to tell this tale. How do ye answer these kinda questions?"

John McCormick, face red, visibly upset and with awesome coolness remarked. "I don't know where you have been this morning. Asleep? Was your father up in Inverness, same time, same place as Peter? Does he have secret information of collusion among merchants to attract tourists? If so, he is duty bound to reveal such collusion to the department that deals with fraud. If he has we have not been made aware of his contribution against fraud. Your statement on his behalf is an insult to these children and their parents who have endured all manner of insults and inferences of deceit. Thank the good Lord for decent folk who hear, consider, and make up their own minds."

But the former elation was gone. Euphoria was replaced by skepticism. The Headmaster was visibly disturbed. He dismissed the students after telling them to be seated until Mr. McCrindle's students made their exit. In fifteen minutes the auditorium emptied. The students returned to their classes. The exhilaration of the moment, dissipated. In its wake, solemn reservation. The excitement and pride that simmered in the beginning assembly was changed to apprehension and suspicison. The negative question put an entirely new feeling into Peter; too new for his young mind to fully understand.

Returning to his class, Ms. Burns, pointed to the black board. "We don't have our math or reading books today. However, I have jotted down some sums for you to copy. Be sure you get your numbers right or you'll be coming up with wrong answers. For your reading assignment, I want a composition from each of you as to what you did on your holidays. I will mark more for neatness and spelling than for content; although content plays a part."

The class proceeded to copy what was on the board until the bell rang for lunch. The period was shortened because of the assembly; but food was needed and time allotted for lunch. Standing in line inside the room, Peter felt his first push. He turned to see who had pushed him, but all eyes were averted; no one acknowledged the incident. When he reached the door a foot shot out tripping him, causing him to tumble into the hall.

"Careful Peter," Ms. Burns scolded, "Don't be in too much of a rush." Peter flushed. He heard titters behind him but again could not pick out the culprit.

The lunch period was filled with small but aggravating incidents. Someone spilled milk on his tray. He was pelted with a bit of ham; snickers haunted him as he tried to keep his cool. He moved to another section but almost tripped on someone's big boot placed in his way. As a rule he enjoyed his bag lunch; today it was difficult to swallow the sandwich his mum had put in. Not one of his chums came around. He saw them in a gang looking his way and smirking. Never had Peter felt so alone. How he wished for someone to clue him in as to what was going on . No one bothered. He was isolated. Friendless.

Jamie didn't look outwardly disturbed. His mannerisms defied the bullies to go too far. When the innuendoes fell flat, not even acknowledged the purpose of upsetting him soon lost its steam. He was a decent lad by all accounts. He was respected by his classmates and teachers alike. He was also their greatest soccer player. They depended on him to win for the school. At lunch, when some tricks were tried and fell back on the perpetrators, there was a shrugging of shoulders and an attempt to get back in his good graces. He pretended nothing had happened but presented a cool demeanor that upset his chums. The rest of the day was uneventful. His thoughts went to Peter and Alison and wondered how they were faring.

Alison, meanwhile was having her own bit of trouble. She was aware of side glances and smirks her chums exchanged. She heard their laughs and recognized the significance. The passing of notes and giggles left her angry. She was disappointed for they came from those whom she had formerly called her best chums. Keeping her head up and writing down the assignment on the board kept her from getting up and going back and bashing them in the face. Alison's temper matched her red hair. She also knew that the best defense was a good offense Alison smiled her sweetest in their direction. She was going to ride their storm. They wouldn't sink her ship but she'd sink theirs.

The first day of school, though shortened, seemed interminably long for Peter. He deliberated whether to ride the bus or walk home. He opted for the bus, figuring he'd be in a safer environment with an adult in charge. While waiting for the bus he was bombarded with "How rich are ye now, wee Peter? Did ye ask Nessie for her autograph? Did your folk get enough for a public education for ye?" On and on went the taunts until the bus mercifully arrived.

In line he was shoved. On the steps he was tripped. The young bus driver hollered at him; "Dinny be in such a hurry, there's room for all."

He sat as close to the bus driver as possible hoping for some protection. Mary Chapman a small, blue eyed, dark haired girl came and sat down beside him. She whispered. "Peter, I believe what you said in assembly. Pay them no mind. They're just jealous because they didny meet oor Nessie. Don't worry things will turn out alright, you'll see."

Peter had to turn away, for these first words of comfort and belief opened up flood gates and he was afraid he was going to cry. This would have jollified his tormentors. In spite of damaged emotions and tattered self esteem, he acknowledged her with a grateful smile.

When the lads in the back seats began their catcalls and rowdiness the driver pulled into a side street and turned off t he motor. "Noo laddies and lassies, I am Ian Fielding and I have all the time in the world. In fact the longer I sit, the longer my run, means mare money in mi pockets. So here's the deal wi' this bus. While I'm in charge if ye get too noisy, I jest pull over to the curb and sit til yer through makin my wee drive difficult. Ye ken where I'm comin' from? So if yer late for yer favorite telly program, put it doon to the rowdies on the bus."

There were no more incidents; no raucous tones no mishaps the rest of t he ride home. Peter could not help smile and say a silent 'Amen' to the wisdom of the young bus driver. One in a thousand. He'd go far in public relations.

Peter's corner was the same as Mary Chapman's and they walked together in spite of the hoots and hollers and catcalls that followed them. He was sorry to part company with her, his first ally.

Coming into the house he put down his school bag and made for upstairs. Agnes, in the kitchen heard him come in and expected him to make his way to the kitchen for his usual after school snack. She heard him go up the stairs. She waited thinking he had headed for the loo. When he didn't come down she sensed trouble. Up the stairs she went and found him lying face down on his bed.

"What's the matter, luv? Was the assembly a bit too much? Peter, look at me when I'm talking to you."

Peter turned to face his mum. She saw pain written on his face. Without another word, she gathered him in her arms and began to rock him to and fro. "There, there, luv, it'll be alright in a wee bit. Things are a bit strange right now, but they'll soon be sorted out and all will be as before."

Peter struggled from her grasp and shook his head. "Mum, it was awful. The fellows don't believe me; they think we got paid to say we'd seen Nessie. They tripped me, pulled my hair and threw food at me in the lunch room. The teacher didny see anything they did. They're so clever. Even on the bus I was tripped gettin' in. Mum I dinna want to go to school anymore. I canny take it." Here he sobbed loudly, letting all the pent up emotion pour out of him like a broken pipe. He continued sobbing until he was exhausted and lay back on his bed.

Agnes wiped his swollen, tear-streaked face with a cold cloth and went down the stairs for something cool for him to drink. She was shaken. Brutality in his peers had not entered her equation of unpleasantness the first day of school. She'd expected innuendoes but not open hostility. She went back upstairs and found him asleep, breathing hard. She covered him with a light cover and managed to get his shoes off. He stirred slightly, but returned to the land of sleep and escape. Oblivion.

She waited by the door for Alison and Jamie. It was an hour before they made their appearance. She ushered them into the kitchen and handed them their after school snack. "How were things with you two?" she queried. Alison blushed a bright pink. "I was the bell of the ball alright; talked about, laughed and snickered at. Oh aye, I always wanted to stand out. Well I did, but not in the way I wanted. I'll opt for ignominy any day instead. Mum, I really wanted to get oot o' my seat and give them a real drubbing. I didny so I had more to me than they did."

Agnes smiled at Alison. "You don't mean ignominy, hen, you mean anonymity. At least you've found that there's a downside to being noticed.

"Jamie how did you fare?" He shrugged his shoulders and bit into a cookie. "It was o.k. in the auditorium until some bloke suggested we were being paid to say we'd seen Nessie."

Agnes looked them in the eye. "Peter's in shambles. He came home and went to his bed. He cried like I've no seen him cry, ever. Apparently he was bullied; pushed, food thrown at him; nasty remarks to his face, and tripped. I am scared for him. He's no as sure of himself as you two. Not taking anything away from what you went through, but I feel you two have a bit more self esteem than your wee brother. I'm wishing your father was home. He'll be fit to be tied and will probably be up on the charge of murder when he hears what they did to his wee lad.

"I still can't figure out those two Headmasters. They were concerned enough ahead of time to take precaution; why didn't they follow up with their concerns?"

"Mum, the lads and lassies waited 'til the teacher was out of sight and out of hearing before they got rough on me. I suspect the same with Alison's bad time." Alison nodded. "So if they were unaware, how could they put a stop to it?" Jamie's reasoning put the problem in proper perspective.

"I know you're right, Jamie. But it doesn't excuse the school because it was ignorant. The Headmasters took time out to assure me that they would look after you. You'll no' convince your father of their innocence."

Alan was home a bit earlier than usual. His first words to Jamie and Alison. "Well, how did the assembly go? Did you have any trouble? Where's wee Peter?"

Seeing their blank looks, Alan knew what their answers were. "Tough going, eh, Jamie, Alison? That's what the chaps at work predicted. Well, it's probably over wi' and yer still in one piece. Where's Peter?"

Agnes pulled at her apron before looking at him. "He's in his room. He's a real basket-case. Everything that could be done to him (within limits) was done. Catcalls, snickers, spitballs, bumps from behind; food thrown at him in the lunch room; tripped several times in the hall and even going up the stairs of the bus."

Alan sat with his head in his hands. All day long he'd worried, wondered and prayed over his bairns. How they were faring. He was disappointed in God for not looking after them better. He soon dismissed that notion as being unfair. People were the perpetrators, they were responsible for their actions, not God. Didn't Job say we had to take the bad with the good? "But" he reasoned, "I'd much rather take all the bad for my family." He knew the folly of that thinking. People grew through adversity. But Peter, he thought, is too wee to face it so soon in life.

Alan went quietly up stairs to look in on Peter. He came down shortly wiping his eyes with calloused hands. "He's so wee luv to be tormented by a pack of ill-bred bairns. I'm calling that Headmaster and givin' him a bit of my mind. First, luv, pour me a cuppa; I sure could use one."

Alan didn't have to call the Headmaster; he was on the line before he sipped all his tea.

"I've been hearing all afternoon of the shameful treatment Peter sustained at the hands of his classmates. A 'wee birdie' brought in the news. I called his teacher and she's dumfounded. Stated she'd not witnessed ill treatment in her class. Perhaps Peter can clear this up as to whether or not he was ill treated behind our backs."

"If you're really interested" (here Alan spoke in proper English which he was wont to use when angry and in control) my son came home in shambles and after sobbing himself to sleep is still upstairs in his bed. He has informed his mother that he does not want to return to school. Oh, yes, it's the truth alright. He was shoved, kicked, punched in the back, for starters. In the lunchroom he was tripped, milk spilled on his tray; food thrown at him along with spitballs. Those were incidental things. The real arrows came wrapped up in words of contempt, labeling him a liar and a charlatan. For the life of me I cannot understand how you educated folk could have missed this. Peter will not be at school tomorrow. Our family Doctor will look him over tomorrow. I understand that you have your hands full, but to let a small boy be persecuted because he told his story, flummoxes me. Remember now, it was at the behest of the school that he told his adventure."

Mr. McCrindle's suggestion was an effrontery to the seriousness of the situation. Alan's face was livid with anger. "No thank you sir. We will not have any social service worker here mucking up things around here. We will rely on our Doctor's prognostication and go with his suggestions. Good day to you sir."

Alan sat back in his chair; anger dissipating. The course of events must be addressed. Anger could wait. Agnes had in the meantime gotten in touch with Dr. Scott McKay's surgery. The Dr. returned their call later that evening. When apprised of the situation, promised he'd make a call the next day. He had been their family Dr. for ages; had delivered all the children and still made house calls.

Peter did not stir from his bed. If he woke it was when members of the family were not in his room; which were frequent.

The phone rang and rang. Calls from anxious parents who'd heard from their children of Peter's ill treatment. They were all so sorry and offered any help needed. They bravely assured the Maitlands that their 'Alice; Sam; Willy, etc' would never have participated in harming 'wee Peter' in any way. Alan and Agnes thanked them for their concern. They un-cradled the phone for peace.

True to his word, Dr. McKay made his appearance the next afternoon. A tall, lanky man with stooped shoulders, he carried the weariness associated with one who was deeply committed to his profession. After consulting with Agnes he went upstairs to examine his patient.

Peter allowed the Dr. to poke at him, look down his throat, peer into the swollen eyes. "Mmm" he began, "seems like you've been in a battle with the old deil himself. Looks like he got the best of you." He chuckled for Peter's sake, but his calm demeanor hid the dismay at finding one so young the victim of emotional trauma. After taking the pulse and getting his thermometer reading; slightly over 100 degrees, it was evident that nothing physical was at work. The Dr. knew that stress could lead to more than physical breakdown. He was concerned as to the lad's mental state.

"Peter, I want you to wash your face and go down the stairs and eat whatever appeals to your fancy. You need to stir around a bit . You must fight back the hooligans that put you here or they'll have won the victory. You're special, that's why they attacked you. You've been set apart and this they can't handle. It makes them all the more insignificant. Now put on your robe and come down stairs. I'm going to talk with your mum and leave something to help you get a good night's sleep. I want you down stairs before I take my leave."

Peter knew directives when he heard them. "I'm just not hungry," he protested.

"Makes no difference. Drink a cup of soup; eat a piece of toast, anything. You must get some food into your body to give it some strength. After that a good bath. That will help you get a good night's sleep. I'll see you downstairs." Peter nodded his head

Advising Agnes against coddling Peter too much he told her of the instructions he'd given Peter. "He's had a bad time emotionally. However, we cannot accommodate it to the extent that the attention will ameliorate the situation. He must fight back now. Don't be too obvious in your concern. Treat him as if he is recovering from a childhood illness, no more than that. This trauma can play havoc on the mind if we indulge in sympathy and concern. Let him eat what he has a mind for; watch a little telly. Keep him home from school tomorrow. Then pray that he's able to face the louts the next day. I'll leave this mild sedative with you. After a good warm bath give him a teaspoon of it. He should have a peaceful sleep."

Waiting until he heard Peter's steps on the stair Dr McKay moved toward the front door. With hand on the door knob, he promised to look in on them the next afternoon.

Seated at the table, Peter toyed with a bowl of tomato soup (his favorite) and saltine crackers. He ate more than he thought he would. Agnes noticed but said nothing. She put down some vanilla pudding by his plate. He glanced up at her and then began to eat it. It seemed to please his taste buds for he ate it all. Agnes was pleased and began to hum. She suggested that he watch a little telly; (something that was forbidden during school days) 'til all homework and dinner was over with.

Peter shook his head; dawdled about the front room then picked up his school bag and went back to his room.

Agnes praised the Lord for giving them such a good physician as Dr. McKay. He had been their fortitude over the years; now he was seeing them through this crisis with calm wisdom.

She sat down wearily on the couch only to be disturbed by the phone. It was Alan asking for news. "Dr. was here and looked him over. He said it's not the physical but the mental that's impaired at this juncture.

He told me not to coddle him and to treat him as if he is getting over an illness. He is to eat what he fancies but he is not to stay in bed all day. He can watch telly if he wants to. He had Peter come down stairs before he left. Peter did eat a little soup and pudding.

"But Alan" and here her voice wavered , "he said we had to watch for signs of depression. He's coming back tomorrow. He suggested I keep Peter home from school one more day. Hopefully he will able to get back to school by the next day. I do feel so much better after talking with him. But he didn't discount the damage that could still be ahead if we're not careful in handling this."

"Hen" interrupted Alan, "I've got to get back to my deliveries I'll be home as soon as I can. The lads here are furious with the situation. I'm so grateful for the support these chaps have shown me. Don't know what I'd do without their encouragement. See you luv."

Peter Falls for Nessie

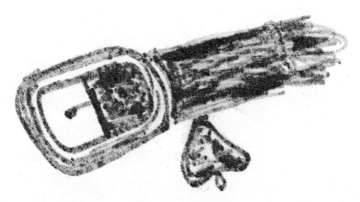

Bit O' Strap

Chapter 7

"Daddy, lookit what I found" exclaimed Tommy McLoud holding up a bit of strap with something dangling from its end.

"Let's have a look" demanded Danny his older brother.

"No, I want to show it to Dad."

Angus McLoud straightened up from his worm digging in the ground near the loch's embankment to view the 'find' of his insistent small son. "Looks like a bit of a strap off some animal, son," he said examining the find.

"Throw it in the loch, it's durty," demanded Danny.

Before the suggestion took root and carried out, Angus McLoud examined the leather more closely. Hanging on the bit of strap was a wee bell. Insight or foresight (as he would later opine) prevented him from telling his son to 'toss the durty thing awa'. Instead he made a decision. "Let's go doon the road to that wee cottage and see the folk what live there. I've a hunch this might be important to them."

"But Daddy, we havny got enough worms yet," whined Danny."

"The day's young yet. Plenty of time to get oor worms."

The door to Dream Cottage opened to the knocking of Angus McLoud. He felt foolish but was not deterred from his mission. He lived in the Highlands and was a newspaper reader. Introducing himself and his lads he explained to the robust man standing in the doorway. "My wee son, Tommy found this when we were digging for worms doon from your cottage. I couldny throw it awa 'til I checked wi' ye to see if this was of any importance to you folk."

Holding out the bit of leather, Sam Maitland took it in hand, then asked the father and sons to come "into the hoose." Sam went to the kitchen sink, got a brush and scrubbed the dirt and sand off the bit of leather and wiped the attached bell. Sam whistled. "Before we go any further sir, would you be kind enough to show me just where ye found this?"

It took a little more than 10 minutes to get to the place where they'd been digging. Sam chortled with glee. "If this is what I think it is sir ye've rescued a wee Glasgow lad from the brink of disaster and reddened the faces of a whole camp of doubters."

"Mary," he yelled,. "come doon and see what these fine folk just found and ye'd best make them a guid cup o' tea. I've got to phone Alex Hamilton to get his long legs oot here."

Mary Maitland was as excited as Sam when she looked at the bit of strap and realized its significance. "Oh, Sam, Sam.....it's the miracle I've been praying for." She set about putting the kettle on for the promised tea. Fixing company tea was the best antidote for covering all emotions.

"I canna find Alex's phone number. Where did it go?" Sam panicked.

"It's under yer nose in the phone stand. Take yer time or ye'll have to wait 'til it finds you," admonished his wife.

After misdialing the number twice, Sam finally got in touch with Alex Hamilton. "Alex, remember me? Sam Maitland oot at Dream Cottage?"

"Now just who could forget such a lovely chap with such a grand disposition. What can I do for you. Have ye been seeing Nessie walk again, or its twin?" Alex laughed at his twisting of Sam's indignation.

"I've something to show you found by a great gentleman and his two braw lads." Sam stated piously.

"O.K. Tell me, Sam. I'm up to my ears in work so make it short and sweet."

"Oh no! If ye want this big, big scoop you come oot here. If ye dinna want to be bothered, there's always yer friendly rival waiting to hear from me. Ye ken the one I mean."

Alex Hamilton groaned. "Yer an old fox; ye know that Maitland. Ye'll no be pullin' me leg?"

"Did yer leg get pulled the last time, laddy?"

Hamilton had to concede that indeed he had not. "I'll be right oot. Better be good, old chum." He rang off.

In as short a time as was humanly possible, Alex Hamilton made his appearance. He bounced up the steps to be greeted by an excited, but self controlled Sam. In the kitchen he met Angus McLoud and his two young boys.

Hamilton got right to the point. "What's this big scoop, Sam? I left a pile of stories to put to bed."

"Well," chortled Sam. "This is a bigger story than any ye've on yer wooden desk." He held up the bit of strap (now scrubbed clean) with the bell dangling. Alex looked quizzically at it and waited for an explanation. He was dumfounded at Sam's perorations.

"Ye ken when Peter was tellin' his story he said the wee sheep had a bell on its neck that rang when the beastie shook it? Well we went to where the Mc Loud lads, digging for worms came up with this, and…"

Alex finished for him. "The place where Nessie went into the loch. Tell me that's where this was found. Go ahead and make my day!"

Sam nodded. Angus McLoud nodded assertively as did his boys.

"Mon, Oh mon," shouted an uninhibited Alex. "Ye ken what this means? This is proof positive of Peter's story. Mon, Oh mon.....what a scoop!" He became sober. "We've got to get more verification. Let's see that strap." Alex took it in hand and searched with his sharp eyes and found what Sam's dimming eyes hadn't picked out. The initials F.S. "Ye know," said Alex as he read out the initials "what these stand for? Frank Stuart the farmer I interviewed about the loss of his sheep." He jumped for the joy a reporter gets when uncovering a story no one but he possesses. "I'll get in touch with Frank and show him this bit of leather and cinch the conclusion we're drawing. I'll have to take this with me. But I'll be on the phone as soon as I get to Stuart."

He put the leather in his pocket and headed for the door. He turned around and said solemnly. "Mr. McLoud, I'm flummoxed that you had the presence of mind to keep this bit of strap. Most people would have thrown it in the midden. It's a bit of a miracle that you came here. The guid Lord is certainly interested in getting Peter off the hook. Now, one more thing, Sam, and you folk as well; can I get you to say nothing about this, not to anyone until it it's verified. If this gets out and its a false lead, it will do more harm than good for Peter."

They gave him their solemn word; delighted at being the possessors of until the all clear signal was given. Alex asked to use Sam's phone.

Hamilton was intent in locating and getting the services of Scott McNeill. When he located Scott he fumed. "Mon, where've ye been hidin' yersel'? Get in yer junk heap and make it oot to Dream Cottage on the double. Make that on the triple. Something new has developed while ye've been playing hooky. No, I'll no be tellin' ye what's new; but it's bigger than the last time ye were oot here." He hung up the phone on an exasperated Scott McNeill.

Alex, Sam and the McLouds left the house and went to where the lads had been digging. "What probably happened" surmised Alex, "the strap came off when the beastie gave the wee lamb one last shake before sliding into the loch. Mon, oh, mon I canna tell ye how much this news will mean to a wee troubled lad in Glasgow. To make it all the more amazing is that you folk bothered yourselves to see if it was important. It's also incredible when you don't know the lad you're helping. That makes the story even more astonishing human interest story."

Sam nodded solemnly. "From what I hear from my brither, Peter's school chums are tormenting him and giving him an awful thrashing. The Dr. has been in to see him and right now he's staying home from school. Bed rest and sedatives is what's keeping him goin. This will change the complexion of things and save the day."

McNeill's car found them. After hearing and seeing the bit of strap, Scott whistled softly. "Let's gie a look at it." Turning it over in his hands, Scott took his camera and photographed the strap from every angle; front and back.

When Hamilton pointed to the initials and the number on the bell, Scott zoomed in for closer view. "What a story! Unbelievable. Here, you folk stand over there and the wee lad who found the strap, hold it up. Now down on you knees where you were digging and point to the place you saw it. Now Dad, you stand over by them and look interested in their find. Now Tommy, hand the strap to your father. Look like you don't know what to make of it. That's it. Now one more picture by the loch where Nessie slid into the water. Fine. That'll do it."

Scott Mc Neill had them head for Dream Cottage and took snapshots of them knocking at the cottage door. Sam positioned himself in the house and opened the door. Another picture was taken. McNeill left immediately having satisfied himself with his shots. "Thanks old chum; Yer a guid friend," he gave Hamilton a knock on the arm. "But don't get the big head noo, I may be callin' ye a midden next week." He laughed; skipped down the stairs and was in his car heading for Inverness before the folk could say their goodbys.

Hamilton took his leave but not without repeating his request that the news not be given to anyone but the Maitlands in Glasgow. "Tell your brother to withhold the news until you hear from me. Then you can give him the O.K. By then it won't matter for the news wires will be singing out this find all over Scotland when I write my wee piece."

He laughed excitedly; shook Sam's hand and Mr. McLoud's. The boys he hugged, especially Tommy. "What an ending to a miserable truncated story."

Away he went.

The McLouds left shortly after having drunk enough tea and milk to last the whole day.

****

"Sam, stop drumming yer fingers on the table. Yer setting my teeth on edge."

"Just let me be. I'm working up a grand sweat waitin' for Alex to call. He's had plenty of time to run doon that farmer what lost the sheep and get his reaction to that bit o' leather. Why doesny he call?"

His wife shook her head in exasperation. "Could be farmer Stuart is on holidays."

"Farmers canna take holidays. Who'd look after their cattle and sheep. Don't be daft. anybody knows that."

Before Mary could give a terse reply the phone rang. Sam jumped for it and shouted. "That you Alex? It's aboot time ye rang back. Mon, oh mon, ye've had me bitin' my nails to the quick. What've ye learned? Oot wi' it man," Sam demanded.

Alex Hamilton's laugh at the other end of the phone was so loud that Mary found herself grinning. He waited a bit, teasing Sam for the news he knew Sam was dying to hear. "Sam, Sam, I had a wee bit of a time tracking down that elusive farmer. He was traipsing from one sheep auction to another. I did finally nab him buying more sheep for his herd."

"I'm no interested in Stuart's buying habits; I'm wanting' to ken whether or not he recognized that bit o' strap. Now will ye quit foolin' and tell me what he said?"

"Well, we didn't discuss its merits until we got back to his farm. He took his good old time examining the strap, then dipped it in some solution and dried it off." Alex knew this was not what Sam wanted to hear. He smiled to himself, knowing Sam was working up a grand sweat.

"Alex, I'm a ver' patient man," Sam muttered between clenched teeth. "But if ye dinna quit this clap trap and gie me a plain answer I promise ye I'll no be gi'en ye any mare stories that make ye prominent in the pen and ink department. Ye ken where I'm comin' from?"

"Now, now, Sam, you've got my attention. Frank Stuart is a very thorough man. The initials he identified as his but something even better. The wee bell after cleaning, revealed the number 4. He then showed me his ledger where he meticulously keeps track of every sheep born or bought in his flock." Alex stopped and smiled with glee knowing full well that Sam was waiting for the punch line. "This collar and the number match up with the sheep he had stolen the night Nessie took her stroll. So, the conclusion is this; the wee lamb Peter saw in Nessie's mouth is Stuart's missing number 4. No doubt at all at all." His laughter sounded like a train coming through a tunnel announcing it carried precious cargo on board.

Sam yelled over the phone. "What took ye so long to disgorge that bit of information? I do believe ye like to see people suffer." On hearing his wife in the background scolding him, Sam back tracked and muttered. "Sorry, Alex, ye're a guid sort of a lad and I do thank ye for following this up."

"Sam," said a mollified Alex. "I'm asking you again to warn the folk in Glasgow to say nothing 'til it reaches the media. It'll save them a lot of aggravation. They've had enough of that already. Good night ol' man." He laughed and hung up.

Sam was immediately on the phone to Glasgow. It was shortly after 9 p.m. After making noises about the family and of course how Peter was, Sam got to the point. "Alan, I ken ye've been havin' quite a time with folk pestering ye and no believing wee Peter; well, ye're all oot of the woods now."

"What do ye mean we're oot of the woods. Nothing has changed here."

"Well, brother, things have changed here that'll scrap any doubt aboot Peter seeing Nessie."

"Back up, Sam. What are ye talkin' aboot; ye're speaking in riddles."

Step by step Sam took Alan through the day's events, beginning with the Mr.Loud's digging for worms; the discovery of the strap, and their ultimate visit to Dream Cottage. "When I answered the door, Alan this chap wi' his two wee boys stood there. At first I thought they wanted the use of the phone. But no, he explained his boys wanted to fish that Saturday morning and went looking for worms.

"I guess what really got me was how easy it would've been for him to just throw that bit o' dirty leather awa'. But he brought it 'cause he felt it was important. Now, Alan, that's awfully uncanny these days. Folk just don't bother about wee things. Mary says he was guided here. I'm inclined to agree wi' her. But I'm no aboot to tell her case she gets to thinkin' she's fey. I got in touch wi the newsman and he got the photographer oot here. Alex got hold of the farmer that lost the sheep. It all fitted; it was his wee sheep Nessie took into the loch." His laugh was uproarious. All who heard it laughed in unison.

"Sam, oh, Sam" Alan interrupted. "Ye'll no ken what this is going to do for Peter. He's been through the mill and we're half out of our minds over him. He's been pestered, ridiculed and taken physical as well as mental abuse under the noses of teachers who dinna have any notion of what's goin on. He's beginnin' to doubt himself about Nessie. He'll probably no believe me so I'll let ye tell him yersel. Hold on and I'll get him to the phone. Incidentally I'll be paying for this long distance call, brither."

He laughed excitedly.

He heard Sam's laugh at the other end and heard him declare. "I'll be sendin ye the bill, brither."

A reluctant Peter was pressed into coming to the phone. His hello was painfully thin.

"Peter," boomed his uncle in his ear, "I hope yer sittin' doon, for ye'll need to be when I tell you my news. And I'm no funnin' wi' the truth neither. You remember tellin' me aboot the wee sheep in Nessie's mouth and hearing the wee bell sound when Nessie shook the lamb? Well, lad, two wee boys out digging for worms uncovered the strap and the bell still on it. Their dad brought them to Dream Cottage to show it to us and ask if it was important! Can ye believe that! Important? Important! Ye remember the newsman, well he came oot, and the photo man. They looked at the strap, and went to the place where the wee lads were digging; right where Nessie slid into the loch. Such a day we've had.

"Alex Hamilton hunted oot the farmer who'd lost the sheep. His initials are on the strap and he has a record of the strap's wee bell. It matches the number of the sheep that went missing the night you saw Nessie stroll.

"Peter, are ye there?"

"Aye, I'm still here Uncle Sam. I'm just thinking about that wee sheep and how pitiful it sounded and how hopeless it looked. I wanted so much to help it but I couldn't do anything. Now just think, Uncle Sam, what that wee sheep has done for me."

Peter began to weep softly; held up the phone to his dad and crept into his mother's waiting arms.

"Sam," said the somber, choking voice of Alan, "I'll never forget this call. Agnes said it would take a miracle to get us out of this mess. This is it. Thank ye my good brother. We'll say nothing. I'll look forward to Hamilton's article. God bless. Guid nicht."

Chapter 8

It was late before bed was mentioned. Excitement pumped everyone up; no one thought about sleep. Sweet reprieve was good to mull over; every angle parsed. Peter remained the quietest. He was reliving his experience and the wee lamb's death.

"We'll never get ready for the kirk if we don't get to bed" Agnes finally stated, firmly. They looked at each other and found common thankfulness. Up the stairs the children went. Agnes and Alan followed.

Sunday brought a decision to keep Peter home. He had slept poorly; tossing and moaning softly in his sleep. Alan took the two oldest children to the kirk by himself.

After she had seen her 'creations' out of the door, she sat down, a cup of tea in her hand. She pondered over the effect the piece of leather would have on Peter's return to school in the morning. He'd not seemed fit to go on Friday. She'd opted to keep him home. There was no doubt that he'd been vindicated. The media's extensive coverage of the McLoud's discovery had put an end to any and all doubt. Her eyes teared at the thought of what that find had done for her family. Truly it was a miracle that had delivered the family from eternal doubts.

After the luxury of a second cuppa (especially on a Sunday morning) she busied herself fixing a special celebration meal for her family. Humming 'How firm a foundation.' She tiptoed up the stairs to look in on Peter. He lay on his back, arms outstretched, mouth slightly open. He was breathing softly. The scene could have been labeled 'Serendipity.'

An old Jewish saying flashed through her mind; 'Endlessly defeated, but never entirely conquered.' She found herself exclaiming out loud. " We Scots have backbones of steel." She felt a little sheepish at her unbidden outburst.

The phone rang as she descended the stairs. She swept it off its cradle. "Mrs. Maitland" a voice inquired. " I wonder if our Glasgow Herald might send out a reporter to visit with your family this afternoon?"

"Sorry" she spoke decisively. "We're giving no interviews , thank you." She hung up before the caller could put in another word. The phone rang and rang; questions thrown at her about the bit of leather; description of the lost sheep. On and on the ringing the phone was incessant. Agnes in desperation removed the instrument from its cradle. Quietness was the fare for the rest of the morning. She finished her dinner preparations.

Shortly after 12:30 her family was home, remarking how good the dinner smelled as they entered the kitchen. After washing up, Alison set the table.

"Peter not coming doon?" asked Alan.

"He was still asleep the last time I looked."

"I'll go up and have a wee look-see."

Alan was soon down with Peter in bathrobe, face washed and hair combed.   Peter smiled sheepishly. "I had a good sleep" he murmured.

"Let's eat" crowed Alan. "Let's stick in 'til we stick oot" he laughed heartily.

"You sound just like Uncle Sam," his children accused.

"Well you know, we were brought up in the same hoose."   He grew solemn , bowed his head to say grace; a different kind of grace. "Dear Lord, we truly thank you for sending along the McLoud family to find what we needed to shut the mouths of doubters. We thank you for giving us back peace of mind and Peter's integrity. Thank you for minding my family. Bless this food. Amen."

It was the best meal they'd had since the advent of Nessie. The phone remained incapacitated.

With dinner over, Sunday chores were dealt with. Peter cleared the table; Alison washed the dishes; Jamie dried them and Agnes put them away. They went into the living room to just talk. There was so much to discuss now that the media was replaying the bit of strap by the McLouds. Scenarios grew like mustard seeds from within and without the television. The endless discussions cleared the minds and gave serenity to the soul now that validation had taken place. Interest in the loch was renewed tenfold.

Around four o'clock the doorbell rang. Alan went reluctantly to answer the insistent ring, ring. He returned with Mr. Chapman of BBC following behind. Mr. Chapman stated the reason for his visit. "I've been in touch with the McLoud family. They have agreed to tell their story as to how they found the sheep's collar, at our studio. We have also contacted the farmer,

Mr. Stuart, inviting him to be there also. He has declined. Now, I would like to have your family appear with the McLouds and put a closure to a most colorful event. We can make the same arrangements; have a car pick you up when the interview time is set. And…"

At this juncture Alan held up his hand. "Thank you sir, but this family will not be interviewed again; certainly not by your station. We came across as bumbling publicity seekers. Your attitude and placating mannerisms only reinforced perception."

"But, but, er…" stammered Mr. Chapman. "You must admit that the story did sound a bit of a stretch. You certainly can't blame the skepticism."

"True, sir, but my family suffered great humiliation because of that interview. It helped to ignite fires of doubt as to Peter's veracity. In no way, sir, will we appear again to get your station off the hook now that proof positive has come to the forefront. I am sorry you came all this way, but the answer now and in the future, is NO."

Chapman left, hat in hand. They stood behind the lace curtains and watched him enter his limousine and drive slowly away down Glamis.

Jamie whistled softly. "He's probably shocked at being turned down. Who turns down an opportunity to appear on the telly?"

"We do" they shouted and clapped their hands with glee. They were proud of their father's ability to speak the King's English with such aplomb and audacity to such an important V.I.P. Their dad was King for a day.

Not daring to replace the offending phone, it remained dislodged from its mooring. Shortly after six the doorbell rang. An irritated Alan went to answer the summons. They strained to hear their father's voice. He returned ushering William Bremner ahead of him. Hat in hand; he was shy and apologized for intruding in the privacy of their Sunday evening.

Agnes smiled and asked if he would like to join them in a cup of tea. He demurred but did not say no.

Around the kitchen table, Bremner said his piece "I was ever so happy to hear of your rescue from the mire of doubt and despair." In this manner he pictured succinctly their situation before the McLouds.. He went on; "You have no doubt been inundated with requests for television appearances; radio interviews; magazine and newspaper insights." He looked at the incapacitated phone and smiled sheepishly. Its truncated condition validated his assessment of the situation.

"I wonder if you would consider giving your testimonies as to how this new discovery has changed your lives. I don't expect you to be ready right away, but I do feel it would be good for your family and put a wonderful closure to this most grueling episode in your lives. I would like you to think it over and get back to me when you feel up to it. You have my home and office number."

He smiled shyly. They returned his smile. They knew they would honor his request.

Alan confessed his reluctance to put his family at risk again. He told of Mr. Chapman's visit and of his, Alan's, refusal to honor the television interview. "He left with the proverbial flea in his ear. Your kindness and deference to us when we were under fire was uplifting and encouraging. It may be a week or two, but we will get in touch with you. Hopefully Peter's ordeal is over."

William Bremner nodded his understanding. After finishing his tea, he took his leave.

'There goes a fine Christian gentleman if ever I saw one" remarked Agnes. Alan nodded in agreement. The phone remained impotent until the next morning.

Later Alan asked "Hen, do you want me to leave the car keys for you. Will you be needing them in the morning?'

"I don't know whether I should drive Peter to school or let him take the bus."

"Mum" said Peter, "I've got to ride the bus or I'll be the laughing stock of the school having to have my mum hold my hand and drive me to the school door."

"He's right, luv. The sooner things get back to normal the sooner the attention will go away." Alan patted Peter's shoulder in agreement.

"Well enough of this palavering, we've all got a busy day ahead. Put out the light and get to bed."

Monday morning came too soon. It was hard to get the children up after Alan went to work whistling 'The Bluebells of Scotland.' Things were getting back to normal she noted as she heard the children squabbling upstairs over their right to the loo. She sighed; not a sigh of irritation rather a sigh of contentment with normalcy.

Agnes packed her 'creations' an extra fine lunch, labeled their lunch bags and set them on the drain board. After a hurried breakfast, a kiss on her check, the clutching of lunch bags, they left the house. She watched from behind her lace curtains as they hurried down the walk, book bags in tow. This was the normal school exodus of past days. She smiled, left the window and poured a comforting cup of tea..

Jamie and Alison left Peter at the bus stop and hurried to their secondary school four blocks away.

Little by little the line grew as the scholars waited in line for the bus. Peter made no comment but nodded when acknowledged by a chum. There was a sense of embarrassment among the boys in line. The girls, however, spoke and gave Peter bright smiles. He acknowledged them without fanfare. He felt as if he were wrapped in a thick, warm anorak; he felt comfortable; without rancor and without an urgency to speak. The tension of that last school day was behind him, the hurt of rebuke was gone. Peter had a sense of well-being; a feeling he'd not had before his humiliation. His self assurance permeated those around him. His former chums had difficulty promoting conversations. Their effort to bridge the gap they'd created left them in a quandary. They felt the difference in the Peter they had attempted to damage. This left them wary and less sure of their footing. The bus finally arrived. Peter sat directly behind the driver. Mary Chapman came in and sat beside him. Her persistent defense of him had created an unspoken bond between them not soon to be forgotten.

The bus driver turned around in his seat and faced Peter. "Well me lad, it's an honor to be drivin' ye to school. I didna believe them when they said ye were makin' up a wee story aboot seein' the beastie. I saw that family what found the sheep's bell and strap. It sure was somethin' how it all turned oot. 'Twas a wee miracle, like my old mom said, 'Somebody up there was lookin' after ye.' Well noo, let's get movin' in the direction of yonder school where yer all goin' to get yersels educated lest ye all end up like me, drivin' a bus full of wee blokes." He shot out into the lane after putting on his signal. He hummed the whole time. The children sat pondering his words and looking askance in Peter's direction. Silence reigned.

SORRY NOTES

Peter looked out the bus window and smiled a smile of sweet revenge.

Peter fantasized his return to the classroom. He would be greeted by a tearful and embarrassed Miss Burns. His classmates would either hang their heads or give him a standing ovation as he entered. None of these scripts were on the drawing board; none played out. Miss Burns standing at the door greeted him pleasantly with a "Good morning, Peter." Some of his chums glanced casually his way; others kept their heads down, deep in the business of seeking wisdom. Missing was the acrimonious air that plagued the room that last school day.

Miss Burns spoke sharply. "Class, come to order." After taking roll call she directed their attention to the blackboard. "Open your arithmetic books to the page noted on the board; copy the sums and be accurate. If you copy numbers incorrectly you will not come up with the proper answers. I'm not pleased with some of your performance in the area of fractions. So we'll have another go at fractions." She was a fair, dedicated teacher who wanted her students to learn to think in her classroom. "Do your sums on scratch paper before putting them in your notebook. If you have any questions raise your hand and I'll come to you. Now get to work."

The rest of the school day was dedicated to taxing the brain. Miss Burns did not let up for a moment. From one subject to another she led them. They caught her enthusiasm for learning and increased their zeal to please her with their output. Much to their surprise their efforts produced pearls of wisdom earned by themselves. Self esteem was legitimately enhanced. Ms. Burns believed that the accomplishment of learning produced permanent self esteem. The lack of knowledge….. low self esteem.

Spelling and composition followed arithmetic. No one asked to be excused to visit the loo. Ms. Burns felt the enthusiasm of her students and was pleased.

Lunch time held no surprise. Peter's chums one by one sauntered over to his table, and without asking, sat down beside him. Little was said, but the breach was filling in; quietly.

They lined up at the end of the day. As Peter passed Miss Burns at the door, she handed him a large manila envelope. He looked up quizzically. "Notes from your classmates" she said softly. Peter's mouth went dry when he saw moisture in her eyes and her nose turning pink. He blushed. "Thank you Miss Burns." She nodded and patted his shoulder. This scenario was far more satisfying that the ones he'd conjured up in his own mind, for this was real. On his way home in the bus with Mary Chapman beside him he wanted to read the notes but decided against it. He felt too many eyes on his back. He'd wait until he was alone. The bus driver gave him a thumbs up. "Well laddie, ye telt the truth there's no denying that. Noo ye can have the last laugh at those what wouldny believe ye. I'm real proud to be drivin' ye to school and back, that I am. I'll be asking ye for yer autograph afore long." He laughed and swung into the street after using his signal. Utter silence prevailed the whole way home.

Coming into the house Agnes, who had been watching behind the lace curtains called out. "How did things go in school today, luv"

"O.K." was his reply as he reached for his after school snack; tossing the large envelope on the kitchen table.

"What's in the envelope, luv?"

"Sorry notes from my classmates."

"Have you read them?"

"No, I didn't want to read them on the bus."

"Well, have some milk with those scones. There's butter and jam on the sideboard. His mum made the best scones. He ate two and drank some milk, then sauntered up the stairs carrying the 'sorry notes'. For a while he lay sprawled on his back reading the notes. Basically they all said the same things. "I'm sorry I didn't believe you when you said you saw Nessie; 'Sorry we gave you such a hard time.' ' I'm so glad that wee chappie found that bit of strap;'… 'My mum said it was a real miracle;'…'I'm sorry', sorry…..sorry."

The notes both cheered and saddened him. Why couldn't his best chums have stood by him?

Especially Danny Snyder, Tommy Nielson, Billy White, just to name a few. Why had they turned against him with the rest. Though their letters were full of remorse it was small comfort for he didn't need them now; he'd needed them then. Peter was searching, like Job, for understanding of a situation he'd never experienced before; rejection; his integrity questioned. He recognized the importance of a person's character. If one were dubbed a liar, and it stuck, there was no getting back a good name. He hoped he'd never be put in another such situation and find his friends deserting him again. Peter's experience with human frailties was a lesson not soon to be forgotten. Insight and preservation of one's good name was the lesson learned and a valuable one at that. Before curling up for a nap he asked himself the real hard question he'd put aside. 'Would he have joined the rest against a chum that was being put down?' He hoped he would have stood alone against the peer pressure; but would he have? He thought long and hard. He recognized the strength of peer pressure. He put it out of his mind lest he come up with an unwelcome answer. Like Scarlet O'Hara, 'he'd think about it tomorrow'. Putting the envelope under his pillow, he turned over, and went to sleep.

Jamie and Alison were soon home with similar envelopes containing 'sorry notes'. They sat in the kitchen eating scones and jam and drinking milk. The topic of discussion was the happenings of the school day and the 'sorry notes'. Agnes laughed at Jamie's terse, derogatory remarks. "They canna even be original; they all say the same thing. I'm sorry, we're sorry, sorry, sorry. No cerebral input."

When Alison began her critical evaluation of the notes, remarking on misspelled words, grammatical errors, etc., Agnes held up her hand. "Now luvs, we've had a bit of a laugh, but in all fairness, these notes are the only avenue your friends have right now to get back their dignity. They're not proud of their behavior and this is the only way they have to put closure to their shame. You know luvs, it's the man in the mirror we have to deal with all the time. Your chums are having a hard time looking the man in the glass in the eye."

Jamie's nature for the most part was one of understanding; one of turning the other cheek. He was incensed at the thought of a few lines of apology getting the students off the hook Not for himself had he grieved. His anger had festered to a boil because of the way Peter and Alison had been treated. He recalled the concern Dr. McKay had voiced to his distraught mom. He voiced his disgust with the offering of sorry notes in exchange for pardon, to Agnes.

"Let it go, Jamie, or the hurt will never heal. It'll fester like a boil and have to be lanced. That will hurt you, not them. The good Book tells us that vengeance belongs to the Lord. He does a much better job of evening things out better than we can."

"I ken you're right, Mum." said a solemn Alison "I'm going to my room and salivate over my sorry notes."

Jamie, not usually vindictive, looked askance at his mother. He sighed. His mother's wisdom had helped him through many a battle. Besides, when he thought of the McLoud family finding that strap and taking it to his Uncle Sam, he knew that was no accident. God had guided them there. He'd let God handle this problem of healing the breach between his chums too. He sighed and went up the stairs slowly. 'Sorry notes' under his arm.

With the children upstairs presumably reading their 'sorry notes' she pealed potatoes at the sink. Rinsing them, she put them in cold water and under a medium jet burner. Returning to the table she sat down with a cup of tea in hand, thinking. She knew where her children were coming from regarding the notes. She empathized with their anger. Her problem was how to defuse the resentment of their anger without minimizing the damage done to their self esteem. Neither did she want to feed their antagonism toward those wanting to make amends.

The notes were gestures of remorse but were they enough? She thought not. Written words of anger or contempt, if not sent were avenues of relief. The writer vented rage on paper not on victim. The spoken word hit its target head on and could never be retrieved. The damage was done; mending was slow in coming to the one receiving the umbrage.

Agnes remembered a story she'd read as an upper-classman. It dealt with an imagined time when cold air was so frigid, that words froze in the air. When the thaw came, a cacophony of words cascaded in every direction finding the intended ears. Now she wondered if some who had spoken harshly wished they'd been more discrete; wished their words had been erased in the air; missing their intended victim.

Her musings were interrupted by the insistent clanging of the phone. Picking up the receiver she barely said "Hello" when a brisk, commandeering voice inquired; "Am I speaking to Mrs. Maitland? Is Mr. Maitland at home? Will you please give him this message from the Lord Provost of Glasgow's office?"

Agnes had no opportunity to answer any rhetorical questions, but she did manage to inform the caller that "No, Mr. Maitland is still at work."

"I am Ms. Farquart, his Honor's secretary. I am instructed to give you the following message: The Lord Provost is declaring the last Saturday of this month as Nessie's Day. We would like your family to be the guests of honor. Please have Mr. Maitland call this office (she gave Agnes her number) when he comes home from work. Thank you for your cooperation. I will be listening for a return call; today if possible."

The phone went dead in Agnes's limp hand.

She mulled over the entire conversation still hanging in the air and sat down in a daze. "Not again" she moaned. Closure had set in . The children were

221

interacting with their chums again. Surely Nessie was fading into semi-oblivion until someone else was unfortunate to encounter her. Agnes was suddenly exhausted. The tensions of the past weeks were finally catching up with her.. How much more upheaval could they as a family endure? It was all she could do to keep from screaming out in frustration.

Jamie came into the kitchen . "Mum," he stated "I'm throwing away these I'm sorry notes. I've read them all; they say the same thing and I don't need them to build up my ego. I want to get on with my life the way it was before Nessie."

Alison soon followed him. Almost word for word she declared she was tired of the notes that said the same things over and over. She too was anxious to get rid of them and back to being normal. "Did you keep any Jamie. Bet you did."

He blushed a bright red and confessed he'd kept a couple.

"Bet I know whose letters you kept," she teased; "Alice Cameron's and Elsie Folk's."

"Well" he opined; "I can guess which boys' letters you have under your pillow right now" he jibed in return.

Alison tossed her head, left the room without answering him.

During the conversation between the siblings, Agnes was quiet. Jamie looked as her and asked the obvious. "Mum is something up? You look like you don't feel good. Can I get you a cup of tea or something."

Agnes looked fondly at her oldest child. He had always been aware of her feelings and had often been the one to whom she confided. She nodded her head and motioned for him to sit down. She told him of the phone call from the Lord Provost's secretary.

"Oh, no! we dinna need any more publicity. Folk are as sick of Nessie as we are. Why can't His Honor leave well enough alone? What will Dad do? He'll burst a blood vessel for sure."

Agnes nodded. Her biggest problem was hitting Alan with the news when he came home from work. She rose from the table and took the boiling potatoes from the burner. She drained them, mashed them, and put them on top of the mince in the casserole for their dinner of shepherd's pie. She asked Jamie to call Alison down to set the table and go and look in on Peter. He went off without a word. She was putting on the tea kettle when Alan came in the back door whistling 'Blue bells of Scotland'.

Pecking her on the cheek he inquired. "Well, luv, how did your creations make out at school today?" She assured him that everything went fine. She told him of the individual packet of 'sorry letters' each had received from class mates. He shrugged dismissively and stated, "Sorry letters won't make up for what they did to oor wains. They should be flogged."

Agnes shook her head impatiently. "You canna expect all folk to feel responsibility for their actions the way we try to encourage our wains to feel. Let it be. Be thankful they were at least encouraged to try to bridge the gap." She turned abruptly away from him and went to the sink. He sensed her aggravation and asked; "What's eating you? If I said too much I'm truly sorry."

Agnes turned and looked at him straight in the eye. "I've something to tell you and I dinna want you jumping down my throat." Alan looked a bit scared and said; " What are ye talking about?"

She spoke firmly and with great deliberation. "The Lord Provost's secretary called today." Alan's eyes opened wide. Before he could say a thing, Agnes held up her hand for silence. "It seems that His Honor is declaring the last Saturday of this month Nessie Day.. We're to be the guests of honor. His secretary was definite about you calling her office when you came home tonight for full details."

"Yer making this up, eh?" He snorted.

"I'm no more making it up than my name's Agnes Maitland. Here's the phone number. Call her. It's no joke and it's not goin' away either from the sound of that hoity toffy-nosed secretary of His Honor's."

With the number in hand Alan was on the phone dialing. In no time at all Ms Farquart was on the line repeating almost verbatim what Agnes had told him. He too, had difficulty getting in a word edgewise.

When he finally did, it was none too complimentary to the request she'd delivered for the Lord Provost. "Tell His Honor we've had enough of Nessie. My bairns have been hooted at, insulted by friend and foe alike. If the City can afford to waste money on such nonsense, they can do it without oor participation. The Maitlands are no goin' to be paraded around Glasgow and made to feel like fools in any celebration. Ye'll have to have your parade without the Maitland family."

Ms. Farquart evidently broke his tirade with astute comments that made his face go from color red to deep purple. The conversation ended with Alan looking at the instrument in his hand, realizing there was no one at the other end. Before he could begin shouting, Agnes raised her hand. "I told you you'd get nowhere with that icicle of a woman. Before you yell at me, tell me exactly what she said that made your face change colors. "She politely informed me that they would have the parade with or without us. The City fathers would look at us as being unmindful and unsympathetic to the plight of downtown Glasgow. The merchants see this as a way of drumming up business for hotels, restaurants and sundry shops. How often does such an event take place and with a lad from Glasgow the hero? They expect to encourage folk to see Bonnie Scotland. Dignitaries from other cities are invited; the Lord Provost of Edinburgh will be one of the speakers, etc., etc. It's going to be one grand affair with floats and all. I'll tell ye what, if we don't participate we'll be in worse shape than we were when nobody believed wee Peter's story. I'm at my wits end as to what to do."

"How did the conversation end?"

"With that cold woman ignoring my babble and informing me that a letter delineating the details would be in oor mailbox in the morning. She will wait for our final decision before getting back to His Honor." Alan finished speaking and reaching for his cup of tea. Head went on his hands. "We're boxed in; we canna get awa from Nessie."

"Let's see what the letter says before we make too much fuss over this," was Agnes's thinking. "It's not going away, that's for sure. But let's not make fools of ourselves before we get the letter." He nodded, then asked; "The bairns, they got along alright in school the day?" She nodded. "They're more like themselves and they seem to have profited by the experience in a way I canna put my finger on. All in all, Alan, they seem to have benefited rather than harmed by what they went through; made them aware of the reality of minds being changed with the wind. I honestly believe they have gained a good lesson in human behavior that they'll not soon forget." She took a drink of tea.

"Maybe," he temporized. "But I canna forget so soon wee Peter's fears and fever. They may forget soon, but it's not goin' to leave my mind any time soon. After all they're my flesh and blood." He sighed loudly and took a gulp of tea. "I'm goin' upstairs to see them."

She sat once more musing and remarked to herself how often lately she'd been forced to 'stand still and wait'. She remembered the Scripture about those who serve by standing and waiting. "I'm the personification of that text. I've had to sit and stand and wait." She shook her head, arose and went to the oven where her shepherd's pie was nicely browning. She went to the stairs and yelled. " Alison, time to set the table. Come doon now, luv."

Nothing untoward happened in the household that evening or the next day. The letter, however, did arrive in the afternoon mail and she debated whether or not she should open it. It was addressed to Mr. Alan Maitland. She took cover in the fact that her name was not on the envelope and that fact fortified her against eagerness to open it. When Alan came in the backdoor his first question was ; "Well, did His Honor send us his letter? Did it come by regular mail or was it hand delivered by horse and carriage?" Agnes's laugh was tremulous. "It canna be too important for it came wi' the rest of the junk mail delivered by oor ain postman." She handed him the letter and stood behind him as he sat at the kitchen table reading it.

The letter was short and to the point. The merchants were endeavoring to increase interest in Glasgow's economy with a 'lad from Glasgow being a proven celebrity'. They intended to use the occasion to drum up business for sagging downtown sales; as well as promoting Scotland to tourists world over. There would be series of fifteen floats; the Maitland family riding on the lead float. They were not expected to be making any speeches; just to be friendly and wave to the crowds.. Dignitaries from Edinburgh, Sterling

Dundee, Ayr , and as far as Oban and Inverness had already booked reservations at happy local hotels. Speeches would be delivered by the Lord Provost of Glasgow; words from the Lord Provost of Edinburgh and others as the plans progressed. All in all the parade and proceedings would take no more than two to three hours in length. The letter concluded with a plea for the family to participate in 'Nessie's Day' as good Scotsmen, for it would be profitable for them and the children. The letter urged an early reply to Ms. Farquart, who would fill them in with more details.

"Profitable for us and the children?" scoffed Alan. "I canna see how that will come about." They mulled over the letter some more. All in all it seemed innocent enough and two to three hours on a Saturday morning wouldn't be too bad. It was easy to waste that much time around the house and still come up with nothing accomplished. "Hen, I have a gut feeling that we'd best join the merrymakers or leave Glasgow." Agnes nodded in agreement.

"It's going to go on with or without us. How could we explain to friends and foe alike if we didn't show up? I hate to drag the children into the limelight again, but they too would be razzed if they were no shows."

"Let's wait 'til after dinner before we discuss it with them." Alan nodded conspiratorially.

Later that evening watching the evening news, Alan muted the telly and cleared his throat. Peter, Alison and Jamie looked in his direction. "It's no good news

I'm about to share, but it's got to come out" said Alan. "And it's no goin' awa."

"What has to come out?" asked Alison looking a bit scared

"It seems that the Lord Provost of Glasgow and the city council have decided to declare the last Saturday of this month, 'Nessie's Day.'"

The children groaned, anticipating something upsetting to follow.

"So bairns, it seems that there will be a conglomeration of floats parading doon toon Glasgow, and we're to be in float number one." He paused and looked at the stricken faces. He sighed and continued. "I ken just how you're feelin' because I feel the same way. But, and this is a big BUT; if we dinna cooperate, we'll be looked at as turncoats. The merchants are going to promote the day to drum up business for the draggin' downtown sales; the hotels will profit by tourists and all in all they're figuring to gain more than they put out on the cost of the parade. The VIP's from Edinburgh and other cities are already making preparations to come. It's also going to promote Scotland's fair hills and heather, and resurrect Nessie to the world at large. So you see, we just canna ignore the request from the Lord Provost's office and get away wi it. Neither your mum nor I are happy about this turn of events, but its oot of oor hands and tied up wi tight rope. Do ye ken what I'm sayin?"

Jamie broke the silence.

"Dad, don't worry about us. After the heckling we've taken, being on display isn't going to be as bad as what we've been forced to take. Anyway, Peter's story has been proven so we've nothing to be ashamed of. We can't be looked at as charlatans or con men anymore. Who knows, we might even enjoy it."

Alison turned to Agnes. 'Mum what should I wear on the float?'

Alan threw back his head and roared with laughter. "It's settled! 'Here we come Maitlands on parade' Alison's set the tone. 'What shall we wear that'll impress the onlookers?' He laughed with relief. Alison's face reddened. She shrugged amiably.

Peter looked a bit flustered. "I guess I can handle being on a float. I've been on one. I won't have to stand too close to the edge? I wouldn't want to fall off and make a fool of myself."

Alan looked at Agnes . "Seems like our children are more pliable to the workings in the field of politics than we give they credit for. They're able to confront new situations with small concerns: what to wear; not falling off the float and concluding that the event would be more enjoyable than what they'd been through. I'd say the Maitland children have faced adversity, overcome it, and advanced to another rung on the ladder of life. We've raised some sturdy bairns, Mrs. Maitland.."

"You just finding that out, Mr. Maitland?"

After the children left for school; books and lunch bags in hand. Agnes had her leisure cuppa. This cup of tea was the most important of the day for her. Her man was off to work; her children off to school, and she had a bit of time just for herself. She enjoyed the luxury of being a stay at home Mum. Finishing her tea and putting the cup and breakfast dishes in the soapy water, she reached for the phone. In a short time, she was speaking directly to Ms. Farquart. "This is Agnes Maitland. Please inform the Lord Provost that we'll be pleased to participate in the parade. Thank him for giving us the honor of being on the first float."

Before she could hang up, Ms. Farquart, after thanking her for calling asked; "Would you like a city car to bring you to the parade?" Agnes assured her that they could make it there on there own. After polite goodbye's the phone went dead..

Agnes went to the sink and sank her hands in the soapy dish water and washed hei morning dishes. She did much of her thinking with hands in soapy water. What would she wear? She laughed aloud. "I'm so much like Alison, or is she like me in the appearance department."

When the Saturday in question arrived, apprehensive feelings well hidden under outward bravado for two weeks rose to the surface. Tensions were so thick no one dared open the subject. No one spoke at the breakfast table as they ate a hasty breakfast. The children were soon ascending the stairs to get dressed.

''Don't spend too much time in the loo'' shouted Alan up the stairs. "Other folk have to preen themselves as well." There came laughter down from above at the thought of their staid father preening himself before a mirror.

The parade was scheduled to begin in front of the City Hall at 10:30 a.m. sharp. Not wanting to get there too early, Alan decided to leave the house at 9:45 a.m. and take his time driving downtown. They still reached City Hall a bit early, but finding their special parking place, they parked and sat in the car feeling like fools waiting for someone to tell them what to do. Finally Agnes suggested they go into the building and wait there.   This suggestion was carried out. Making their way up the wide stone steps to the front door, they were greeted by a young woman in a beautifully tailored dark green tartan suit. Extending her hand she exclaimed; "Good of you to come a bit early. I am Elsie Farquart and 1 can give you a few details before the floats arrive." She glanced at her tiny wrist watch and murmured "Follow me; I believe the Lord Provost is in his office. He asked to meet you as soon as you arrived."

Leading the way through City Hall, they climbed beautiful marble stairs flanked by dark mahogany stair casingsto the second floor. Stopping at an impressive door marked Angus Campbell. Lord Provost. Glasgow, Ms. Farquart turned the brightly polished brass handle and opened the door.   She led them through the outer office into a hallway and stopped at a door marked PRIVATE.   She knocked lightly; listened for a 'Come

in' and led them in to the august place of business of
the one who ran the City of Glasgow. His Honor was
seated behind a large kidney shaped desk, in a dull red
leather chair. He swiveled and rose, as he surmised the
identity of his visitors. The Lord Provost was robust
looking man with sandy hair mingled with silver. He
held out his hand in greeting. "This" directing his
glance at Alan, "is the father of our Glasgow lad who
saw our Nessie."

Alan felt like Livingston, discovered by Stanley.
He nodded and shook the proffered hand. He then
introduced Agnes, Jamie, Alison and finally Peter. Alan
was aware that he sounded terse, for his resentment
at his family being invaded once again surface. "My
children seemed to feel the event would do them no
harm. Peter's a bit afraid that he might fall off the
float, and my wife and I are looking forward to the day
being over and getting back to being as normal a life, if
possible, that we had before Nessie entered our lives."

If His Honor was perturbed by Alan's curt,
forthrightness he covered it well. "I can well understand
your sentiments completely. But as true Scots you
canna ignore the significance of what this sighting to a
Glasgow lad means to all of us here in Glasgow. Man.
oh man, all of Scotland spits on our city; considers us as
at the bottom of the barrel as far as class is concerned.
With this event, other cities, especially Edinburgh
has to give us a second look. Glasgow has great
universities; excellent hospitals and grand forbearers
. All that's been lost by the rowdy bums who keep
making headlines by their hooliganism. Now that we

have someone to point to, someone the guid Lord sent Nessie in front of, ye canna let the opportunity go by to see another side of Glasgow's good folk. We're having an opportunity of rubbing other cities' contempt for us in their faces. Beside helping economically, do ye ken now why I'm doing what I'm doing?" His Honor donned a most pious look.

They sat in a waiting room down the hall until Ms. Farquart came and escorted them down the City Hall steps to the waiting number one float. There were no surprises about what it would look like. A huge replica of Nessie was their magic carpet. Its head turned right and left; hanging from its mouth was a wee paper-rmache black and white sheep. The whole effect was so realistic that Peter gave a little gasp when he first saw it. There were seats under the neck of Nessie and the Maitlands positioned themselves there. Before the parade began, others joined them on the first float, sitting around the edges, legs dangling over the sides that looked like the loch's embankment.   Alan had to acknowledge that it was truly a piece of ingenious art. "They can say this for the folk of Glasgow." he murmured to Agnes, "they're as clever a bunch of folk as any the world over." "Aye," Agnes murmured back. I felt that about our attitude when the Lord Provost was talking about the reason for this parade.

"Och aye," her husband remarked, "but don't forget, hen, he's a formidable politician. He didna become Lord Provost by being a bleeding heart. He's a shrewd Scot underneath that smarmy smile. Merchants will be ringing up plenty of pound notes in their tills by nighttime. But I hadny thought of the impact on Glasgow's image. That was no phony pitch he flung our way. I'm glad we came." Agnes reached over and patted his hand.

Katie S. Watson

Chapter 9

The Maitland family watched as the chairs were placed on the speakers' platform to the right of the City Hall steps. Dignitaries would be sitting on them following the parade of floats around the main section of downtown.

The school bands were there in their school tartans. A bonny sight Agnes thought. She was getting into the festive mood. She glanced at Alan and found him looking with guarded pleasure at the happenings. Jamie was enjoying it immensely. Alison sat upright trying to look lady-like, and Peter's eyes were everywhere; taking in the goings on. " Yes," she reflected "It had been the right thing to do. We Scots are a proud people and we band together for a common good."

The tall impressive Head Major swaying in his kilts began summoning attention with his wand and the pipers tuned up. As the bagpipers took to wailing their Scottish tunes, the crowd radiated with national pride.

No greater music to the Scotsman's ear is the sound of bagpipes.

Their float began to move, pulled by a large pickup truck. They glided down the main street lined with sightseers. The people cheered as they came; some shouted to Peter. He blushed. There were banners in the crowd showing drawings of Nessie and Peter. The Maitlands felt the warmth they'd missed when skepticism entered the picture. Alan brushed away uncommon tears and looked over sheepishly at Agnes. "It's a braw day, eh hen?" He grabbed her hand and held it tight. "Aye, that it is" she whispered back. Looking back at the children, they saw excitement and undisguised happiness engulfed them. Bewilderment was present as they realized that this was happening to them. Bonhomie in evidence everywhere.

On and on they glided past crowds of people. Everyone seemed to be in an expansive state of happy anticipation. No scowls seen.

Finally the parade returned to the speakers' platform where a group of dignitaries were seated. Lord Provost of Glasgow escorted the Maitlands to the platform amidst the roars of the crowd. They sat in designated seats. The Right Honorable Provost of Edinburgh addressed the crowd and pointing to the Maitlands remarked. "The only thing wrong with this parade today is that it should be happening in Edinburgh. I'm a wee bit envious that the Maitland lad hadn't hailed from Edinburgh. But we'll forgive his parents for that." The crowd hooted and booed at the thought of Edinburgh being the recipient of such an honor. Glasgow's Lord Provost was the last to speak. He looked at his watch and remarked that all Scotsmen were mindful of their stomachs and he would be mindful of that fact and speak fast and make it short.

A "Hear, hear," came from the crowd.

After the perorations from Glasgow's Provost; which included gratitude to the Maitlands for coming and extending thanks to the McLoud boys up Inverness way; "Who could not be with us, but we've not forgotten them for finding the 'wee bit o' strap,'" he continued. … "It's one thing to say thanks; it's another to show it. The City Council and I have had our heads together for a few weeks and have come up with a solution." He turned and asked Jamie, Alison and Peter to come and stand before him. He then proceeded to put into each hand a document and stated.

"This is a document of education; a guarantee for each of you to attend the university of your choice at the behest and expense of the City of Glasgow. This is in recognition of your fortitude, in spite of disbelief regarding Nessie's walk. No matter who sits in the Provost's office or on the City Council, each document is guaranteed with an unbreakable commitment. And may each of you make the best of this gift. God bless."

The crowd erupted with cheers and hoots of approval.

Agnes and Alan sat dumbfounded; tears coursing down their cheeks when the words resonated through their minds. No more worry about university fees. Unbelievable. This matter had plagued them, most especially as Jamie grew older and would be the first to need their help. Now that burden like Christian's was taken from off their shoulders. The load was laid down. The realization was overwhelming; it was fact, not fantasy. The Lord Provost's word was his bond; no matter who sat in that office.

Turning to Alan and Agnes the Mayor asked them to come and stand beside him. "Now" intoned His Honor. "I've someone here that's anxious to join in the festivities. Turn aroon." They turned and saw Sam and Mary coming down the City Hall steps. Sam all dressed up and Mary's face beaming like a light bulb all dressed up like a Christmas package. They gasped and soon the brothers and sisters- in- law were hugging one another and crying at the same time.

"We had quite a time getting Mary Maitland on oor plane," remarked the Provost. "She had to examine the engine itself before she'd board. The pilot said she even kicked the tires. Well for each of them, we have a package tour of all of Scotland and Wales to be used in their own time table. And, yes, Sam, we're paying for that plane trip here. I see yer a canny Scot like mesel." The crowd went wild. Scarcely had anyone heard the Lord Provost speak in his native tongue or seen this jocular side of him.

A bouquet of flowers was placed in each lady's arms. Sam and Alan were asked to say a few words. They did; very few. Sam said he wasny much of a talker but did thank His Honor and the guid folk o'

Glasgow for taking care of the wee lad who'd been given a hard time. Alan was too choked up to say much, just that this was the greatest day in his family's life. "I've always known I was lucky to have been born in Glasgow; this day proves I was so right. I canna say thanks enough to the Lord Provost. I still have to pinch myself to make sure it's no dream, I'd better stop or I'll begin greetin' and make a fool o' mesel." He shook the Provost's hand and handed back the cordless mike then stopped talking.

The parade over, the Maitlands clasped hands after hands of those on the platform, then descended into the crowd and were pressed for handshakes and good wishes by the spectators. They headed for their car and gratefully pulled away, everyone waving excitedly. Sam and Mary followed in a city car.

Reaching 7 Glamis, they were relieved by the absence of people at their door. Sam and Mary behind them mounted the steps with them.

The women went into the kitchen to put on the kettle. The men found a spot away from the television and talked their 'men talk'. The children searched the telly for reviews of the parade. Each was in his/her own element of exhilaration and excitement. Agnes took the prized documents from each child's hand and examined them in the kitchen with Mary.

"I canna believe it," she repeated over and over. "No more straining the paycheck for an extra pound to put away for Jamie's schooling. I keep pinching myself to see if it's no a dream."

"Aye" remarked Mary. "It's a miracle that's happened and don't you forget it. The guid Lord has poured oot His blessings on yer head lass. I couldny be happier if it was happenin' to mesel."

They hugged and went about making the tea. With the table set and sandwiches and scones on the table the others were called.

It was a happy meal. Laughter and excitement exploded over the simplest of remarks. It had been a long time since Mary and Sam had visited their home so they were doubly blessed that afternoon.

The folk separated themselves and Mary and Agnes were once more alone; clearing away and doing the dishes. And talking. Mary was excited about their tour package and at the same time demurred about leaving her cottage for a week. "I dinna like to leave the hoose too long; never know who'll take a fancy at visitin' without invitation."

"Och Mary, ye canna let a wee fear like that keep ye from enjoying the blessing the guid Lord has given you."

"Aye, lass, I ken yer right. We'll probably wait 'til Spring; then we'll come aroon yer way and visit ye then."

"Well we'd be upset if ye didna do that," warned Agnes.

Too soon the city car was at the door to take Sam and Mary back to the hotel near the airport for their early morning flight. Tearful goodbyes were said; hugs exchanged and promises of soon getting together uttered.

Jamie, Alison, Peter, Agnes and Alan waved from the front porch as the car glided slowly down the street. They waited until they could see the car no longer then sauntered into the house. It seemed so empty.

The rest of the evening was spent channel searching for glimpses of the parade; and of themselves. Several stations carried snippets of the event. They glowed inwardly as well as outwardly as they watched themselves 'on parade'.

Viewing again the Lord Provost presenting them with their certificates of higher education, brought tears, elation and silence. They were so touched; even Peter whose educational needs were far in the future. It was a monumental event for this hard-working family. They would live and relive it many times over.

"Time to get yer baths, then to your beds. "Tomorrow's Sunday." Alan broke the reverie with practicality.

"Alison, your hair needs a good wash. Don't stint on the shampoo. I'll be up later to check if it needs another rinsing. If there's ironing to be done, set it aside and I'll see to it when I come up to tuck you in." Agnes shooed them up the stairs.

Left alone, they went back to the kitchen table for their last cuppa before tending to the chores of getting ready for the kirk.

Alan was the first to speak. "Ye know hen," he said over his teacup "I'd been asking aroon aboot a second job week-ends, but so far none had opened up. I really was afraid we'd have to put Jamie on hold 'til we could get his tuition saved."

"Aye, and I've been searching the papers for jobs for housewives with no marketable skills. There are some out there but too far away. I'd have to get a car and that would defeat the purpose of saving money." She shook her head. "I just canna believe it. Surely the City won't go back on its word, eh?"

"Now hen," he scolded. "Is that the way the guid Lord works? O ye of little faith."

Agnes glared at him. "I wasn't doubting the Lord, Alan only the politicians. Anyway, I'm taking the certificates to the bank Monday morning for safe keeping."

Alan laughed and grabbed her hand. "I suppose you just might get the bank lawyer to look them over for loop holes?" He laughed uproariously.

Agnes smiled an enigmatic smile. "Now, who's tempting fate?" She put their cups in the sink. "I'll wash them in the morning. I've got to see after Alison's hair rinsing. She doesn't get all the soap out of it. Turn out the lights will ye luv?"

She made for the stairs and looked at the green threadbare carpeting and made note to see how much it would cost to re-carpet the stairs. She felt free. Free from educational bondage that had nagged at her for so long. The worry was gone. She hummed softly "Amazing Grace."

Alan followed after her putting out the lights. He took the stairs two at a time whistling 'Bluebells of Scotland'.

A good omen thought Agnes. 'Amazing Grace' over the 'Bluebells of Scotland'. They were blessed. They had a God who knew their needs and supplied them. Bountifully.

Katie S. Watson

Epilogue

Gil and I 'piped' in to our
50th wedding anniversary

As the story develops, faith comes into play. The solution is taken out of Agnes's and Alan's hands. Confirmation, and end of doubt concerning Peter's encounter with Nessie, comes from a bit o' strap found and miraculously delivered to Uncle Sam.

I hope you enjoy this little story. If you do, it has been worth the work and hair-pulling I've done to get it to the printer.

Long ago; far away
(back row) Timothy, Rebecca
Gilbert (holding Mark) Phillip
Thomas, Stephen, Katie (holding Mary)

This story developed as it went along. My interest in Nessie was born while attending Eastern Michigan University. One of my chosen papers was the Scottish legend concerning the 'monster' presumably living in the loch;

My paper on Nessie took on new meaning; keeping in mind the slides, photographs and moving objects recorded by the dedicated 'Nessie' watchers who manned their cameras around the clock in search of a glimpse of elusive 'Nessie'. We were privileged to see the Boston scientists with their yellow submarine plumb the murky waters of the loch with their sonar equipment. The locals had a holiday over the event. Impressive equipment; impressive findings.

As Sam observes in his dialogue with Peter, 'If you visit the Loch Ness Monster Investigation Bureau and go in doubting; you probably will come out doubting. If you go in a believer you will come out more convinced.' It is an exciting enigma that defies attempts of annihilation. It will not go away. It engenders excitement and keeps the adventurous spirit in most people, alive.

I have included a thumb nail sketch of the legend, and a brief overview of Scotland as a country and how it is governed.

Pictures have been included of my parents; Sam and Mary McNeill (Auntie Mary and Uncle Sam) in the story. Also included are pictures of (almost) all the great grand children.

Views of the loch and Scotland as seemed fitting for the story are included

Katie

LOCH NESS, THE LAKE AND THE LEGEND

At a little past noon on a summer day in the forty-third year since Mrs. Spicer shrieked at what she saw, thereby startling her husband, George, I looked out on the waters (dark they were, like iodine) of Loch Ness, and there before me…

But first let me tell of the circumstances that brought me to those shores in the melancholy Highlands of Northern Scotland.

The legend of Loch Ness has in recent times uindergone the most serious and skilled investigations in 1,400 years---since the time when, as the story goes, St. Columba commanded a 'fearsome beastie' in the waters to back off and behave itself. The past summer was a particularly busy season there. From Inverness to Drumnadrochit, and on south to Fort Augustus, scientists were at work to find something outsize and alive in that largest of the British Isles' freshwater lakes.

It involved much more than simply watching and waiting. They positioned highly sophisticated camera gear below the surface. They played recorded beeper sounds meant to attract even the most elusive of lake life. They set sonar to work, scanning the cold depths. They used mathematics and physics and electronic wizardry.

And when the summer ended---when they returned to their universities and laboratories---the legend had been invested with, if not reality, then a certain kind of respectability.

I was there to observe the search, and, in truth, I went in the loch. Not that I believed in the existence of such a creature, and not that I disbelieved. Rather, standing beside those fabled waters, my thoughts teetered on a line of slack skepticism.

There were other observers the Camerons, the Campbells, Mackenzies and MacDonals, Mac this and Mac that---the good people of that good land, Highland born and Highland reared. Well, there were some among them who wouldn't have been surprised had something turned up. That's because they say they've seen the animal.

Alex Campbell: 'It was mid-May, 1934. I was looking across the water and, heavens, there was this terrific upsurge about 200 to 250 yards distant. And then this huge neck appeared, six feet at least above the water, with a small head that kept turning nervously. Oh, the head was just going. I said, 'This is 'Nessie.'

****

To fathom the mystery of Loch Ness, Scottish divers plumb the cold, murky waters of Urquhart Bay---recent hub of scientific activity to either prove or dispel as myth the existence of the loch's fabled monster. Though Highland lore has it that monster bones lie moldering in the waters below Urquhart Castle, they have been as elusive as the creature itself.

By   William S. Ellis & David Doublet

COMPUTER JOINS LOCH NESS HUNT

New York Times Service---As summer returns to the Scottish Highlands so have the searchers returned to Loch Ness in t heir quest for the monster alleged to dwell in the deep and dark waters.

A 1977 expedition to Loch Ness sponsored by the Boston based Academy of Applied Science, will use computer-operated under water cameras to monitor the waters for any sign of large creatures. Divers will also be sent down to inspect objects located during last year's sonar reconnaissance.

Dr. Robert H. Rines the Boston lawyer and Loch Ness Explorer described these plans in an interview before leaving for Scotland last week " In the next few weeks," Dr. Rines said, "the expedition will concentrate on diving operations." Archaeologists from the University of Strathclyde in Scotland and divers from Underwater Instrumentation, a British company, plan to investigate what appear to be ancient stone rings in the shallow north end of the loch.

When the rings showed up on the sonar images last summer experts speculated that they might be ceremonial artifacts of Celtic tribes.   The stones, according to the speculation, were erected before the land subsided and was inundated. If so, they should have been undisturbed over the centuries, which is not the case for most of the stone circles found elsewhere in the British Isles.

SCOTTISH GOVERNMENT

Scotland is part of Great Britain, a constitutional Monarchy. Queen Elizabeth II, is the head of state, But a Cabinet of government officials called Ministers actually rules Britain. The Prime Minister is the chief official. Parliament makes the laws of Great Britain. It includes the House of Commons and the House of Lords. Members of the House of Commons are Elected from the four countries of Great Britain. Scotland elects 72 of the House's 650 members. The House of Lords has limited power. Most of its members are nobles who inherit their seats. Scotland's chief administrative official is the Secretary Of State for Scotland. This official is appointed by the British Prime Minister and is a member of the Cabinet.

Scotland's flag is called St. Andrews Cross.

Scotland covers about a third of the Island of Great Britain. England, and Wales are also on the island. Scotland has a population of about 5 million. About three-fourths of the people live crowded in Scotland's

Central Lowlands, a region that makes up only about a fifth of the country's area. About a fifth of the people live in the rugged Highlands, which covers the northern two-thirds of Scotland. Less than a tenth of the people live in hilly Southern Uplands, which occupies about a seventh of the country.

Scotland has several cities with populations of more than 100,000. Glasgow, the largest city, has about 734,000 people. About 440,000 people live in Edinburgh, the country's capital.

Language; English is the official language throughout Great Britain. In Scotland, English is spoken in a variety of dialects and with a variety of accents. About 80,000 Scots speak Gaelic, an ancient Celtic language. Most of these people live in the Highlands or on Scotland's numerous offshore islands.

Way of life; Most Scottish people live in industrial Cities and towns. Most Scots dwell in small houses or apartments, about half of which are owned by local governments. Many Scottish families, like people everywhere, spend the evening watching television. Scotland receives programs from the British Broadcasting Corporation (BBC) and three television companies under the jurisdiction of the Independent Broadcasting Authority (IBA), and television owners must pay yearly license fees. The fees help finance the BBC, which does not have commercials. The three independent companies—Border Television, Grampian Television, and Scottish Television—broadcast commercials, but advertisers do not sponsor programs.

Scotland has cool summers and cold winters. As a result, many people wear warm tweed suits and coats and thick woolen sweaters the year around. Most of their clothes come from Scotland's famous woolen mills.

Traditions. Most Scottish traditions began with the clans. The clans are made up of families who have a common ancestor and the same name, such as MacDonald; MacGregor; MacLeod' McNeill; McKay. The clans began in Scotland hundreds of years ago. They were organized under chieftains and became known for their feuds. Today, the clans have little importance in the life of the members. Each clan is still headed by a chieftain, but the chieftain is mainly symbolic and has no real authority over the members of the clan. The most famous feature of the clans is their plaid kilts. Each clan has its own plaid design called a tartan. The tartan is used for shirts, ties, other clothing as well as kilts. Another highland tradition is the famous bagpipe. This musical anomaly (often called a windbag) along with the kilt is identifiably Scotland's badge of distinction.

A SEASON OBSERVED

Trees are trimmed; the carols are being sung, Mantels are waiting, for the stockings to be hung. The air is now stirring with excitement and joy, As stores fill with shoppers looking for toys.

There's a hustle and bustle characteristic of the season, As more and more observe it, disregarding the true reason.

In Christmases past, reading scriptures was a passion, And like other traditions, this too, has become 'old fashioned.'

A season is observed when you hear someone say, 'Seasons Greetings to you, and have a nice day.'

They smile and appear to be full of 'good cheer.' And as Christmas approaches, they add 'Happy New Year!'

How empty they'll be, after all of their planning, For in observing the season, they have no understanding.

It is more than a season, it's remembering the day,
When God manifested His love in a sacrificial way.

So Merry Christmas I say, taking note of the reason,
Observing Christ's birth and not another season.

Mary W. Pew

The Boy in the Train

Whit wey does the engine say 'Toot-toot?
　　Is it feart to gang in the tunnel?
　　Whit wey is the furnace no pit oot
　　When the rain gangs doon the tunnel?
　　What'll I hai for my tea the nicht?
　　A herrin' or maybe a haddie?
　　Has Gran'ma gotten electric lickt?
　　Is the next stop Kircaddy?

There's a hoodie craw on yon turnip raw,
　　Ab' sea gulls, six or seven.
　　I'll no fa oot o' the windae Maw
　　It's sneckit, as sure as I'm leevin'
　　We're in the tunnel…we're a' in the dark
　　But dinna be fricket, Daddy.
　　We'll be soon comin' to Beveridge Park
　　And the next stop's Kirkcaddy.

Is yon the mune I see in the sky?
　　It's awfu' wee and curley.
　　See there's a coo and a cauf ootby,
　　And a lassie pulln' a hurly.
　　He's chuckit the tikets and gien them back,
　　Sae, gie me my ain yin Daddy.
　　Lift doon the bag frae the luggage rack
　　For the next stop's Kirkcaddy.

There's a gey wheen boats at the harbor mou
　　And eh' dae ye see the cruisers?
　　The cinnamon drop I was suckin' the noo
　　Has tummelt an' stuck tae ma troosers…
　　I'll sure be ringin' ma Gran'ma's bell

She'll cry 'Come ben, my laddiew.'
For *I ken mysel' by the queen-like smell,*
The next stop's Kircaddy.
Mary Campbell Smith
(From a book of 20th century Scots Verse)

Youngest Grandson
Cameron

1. Inverness Station Lobby
   (author stands under
   'Meeting Point')
2. Departing from Inverness
3. Arriving, Glasgow
   Queen Street Station

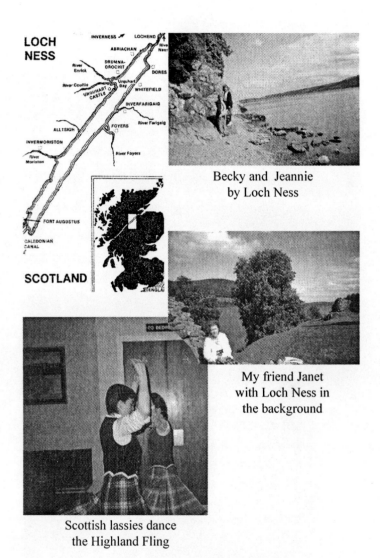

Becky and Jeannie
by Loch Ness

My friend Janet
with Loch Ness in
the background

Scottish lassies dance
the Highland Fling

Around Loch Ness
Scenes from Urquhart Castle

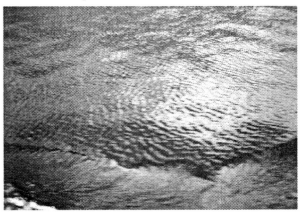

Kimsul Castle
(Clan McNeill)
Isle of Barra

Castle wall armor

Minister/
parishioners
Isle of Barra

Seal MacNeil
Of Barra

Sam and Mary 50th wedding anniversary

Parents of author

William Brenner
(author's great grandfather)

Sam/Mary and wee Mary

Alloway Parish Church

Sister Mary looks
at 'Greyfriars Bobby'

Robert Burns 1759-1796
Scotland's poet, the son
of a poor farmer and a
farmer himself, was born at
Alloway, in Ayrshire, in 1759
in a small cottage which is a
place of pilgrimage to many
thousands of people each
year. His romantic verses
and the poems which reflect
his love of the countryside
are still read and quoted all
over the world.

Burns' Cottage

Sister Jean snaps
photos at Stirling
Castle

270

Highland cattle 'muckle coo'

Stakis Station Hotel/Ayr (Formerly known as Ayr Railroad Hotel; Greatgrandfather William Bremner worked on the railroad at one time)

A church for those on holiday reads the sign (note: it is a baptist church)

We stop for a 'cuppa'

ABOUT THE AUTHOR

Story telling time; Pickens, S.C.   Katie holding Maggie

Born Catherine Scott McNeill, in Glasgow Scotland. With her parents and 3 siblings she immigrated to America.   The family settled in Detroit, Michigan Catherine later met and married Gilbert Hinton Watson in 1939. Seven children were born to this union. Gilbert became an ordained Baptist minister; finishing seminarian training in Fort worth, Texas.

In 1969 Catherine applied and was accepted as a freshman student at Eastern Michigan University.   Graduating with a Bachelor degree in education, she worked in the Detroit Public Schools. Continuing her studies at Wayne State University she earned a Masters' degree in Library Science.   As a librarian she continued working with the Detroit Public Schools until her husband retired to South Caroline in 1985. For a few years she worked for South Carolina Schools as a 'homebound' teacher.

Story telling has been a part of her life's fabric. Reading is a necessary ingredient in the daily calendar. An enthusiastic traveler, she has visited many countries in Europe and the Middle East. Her first publication was a journal delineating the joys and ordeals experienced during their 'church planting' ministry. Gilbert <u>passed away May 13,1992.</u>

Katie and Gilbert

Printed in the United States
37062LVS00001B/37-54